deep water

PETER CORRIS is known as the 'godfather' of Australian crime fiction through his Cliff Hardy detective stories. He has written in many other areas, including a co-authored autobiography of the late Professor Fred Hollows, a history of boxing in Australia, spy novels, historical novels and a collection of short stories about golf (see www.petercorris.net). He is married to writer Jean Bedford and lives in Sydney. They have three daughters.

PETER CORRIS

deep water

A CLIFF HARDY NOVEL

ALLEN&UNWIN

Thanks to Jean Bedford, Jo Jarrah and Robert Hawkins

First published in 2009

Copyright © Peter Corris 2009

Allen & Unwin
83 Alexander Street
Crows Nest NSW 2065
Australia
Phone: (61 2) 8425 0100
Fax: (61 2) 9906 2218
Email: info@allenandunwin.com
Web: www.allenandunwin.com

National Library of Australia
Cataloguing-in-Publication entry:

Corris, Peter, 1942– .
  Deep water / Peter Corris.
  ISBN: 978 1 74175 677 7 (pbk.).
A823.3

p. vii Lyrics by Richard Clapton, reproduced with permission of Mushroom Music Publishing
p. 111 Lyrics by Don Walker, reproduced with permission of Universal Music
p. 185 Lyrics by Bob Dylan, reproduced with permission of Sony Music

Set in 12/14 pt Adobe Garamond by Midland Typesetters, Australia
Printed in Australia by McPherson's Printing Group

10 9 8 7 6 5 4 3 2 1

*For Drs Sean Kristoffersen, Glynis Ross,
Patrick Groenestein and Michael Wilson,
with heartfelt thanks.*

Deep water—I'm caught up in its flow.
If I'm in over my head, I'd be the last to know.

Richard Clapton

part one

1

I woke up in an intensive care unit in San Diego, California. It was a beautiful day—the blue sky San Diego was famous for filled the window. But any day would have been beautiful because I was alive.

'Mr Hardy,' the tall, tanned man in the white coat said, 'how do you feel?'

'As if I've been hit by a truck. What happened?'

He reached for my hand and shook it in a firm but cautious grip. 'I'm Doctor Henry Pierce. I'm a cardiac surgeon.'

'Yes?'

He flipped through some notes in a ring-bind folder. 'It seems you were walking along *our* pier—' he said it the way a Sydneysider might say *our* harbour bridge—'and you bent to pick something up, or move it aside.'

'I remember. A box of bait,' I said, 'heavier than I expected.'

'You stood, shouted and then fell headlong. You suffered a head wound but, more importantly, a massive coronary occlusion.'

I heard what he said, but I was groggy, with some pain

and discomfort in my upper body, and I had trouble taking it in. 'I was looking for Frankie Machine,' I said.

'Excuse me?'

I sucked in air with some difficulty, as if my ribs were preventing me from filling my lungs, but I grasped his meaning. 'Doesn't matter, Doctor. A heart attack, you're saying. What am I looking at—medication, that balloon thing and the bit of plastic?'

He smiled. Dr Pierce had the sort of urbanity that goes with skill, success and money. 'Mr Hardy,' he said, 'you've already had a quadruple heart bypass procedure.'

Over the next few days, Dr Pierce, cardiologist Dr Epstein and a nurse helped me to piece it together. I'd been very lucky, especially considering the strictures of the US health system. One, I'd been carrying my passport and my wallet with a fair amount of cash in it, a Wells Fargo ATM card and a card showing my top level of medical insurance in Australia. Two, an off-duty paramedic had been fishing near where I fell and knew what to do. He got my heart started and I was in the hospital hooked up to machines within half an hour.

The diagnosis was unambiguous: a major blockage in a crucial area. My daughter Megan's name was in the passport as the person to contact in an emergency. They called her. I wasn't in a condition to sign consent forms, immunity undertakings, stuff like that. They got her OK, prepared me, took a punt on things like my susceptibility to medications, unzipped me and got to work.

'It was a four-hour operation,' Dr Pierce said. 'Pretty simple really, and very satisfactory. I was able to use the two arteries in your chest, which gives the grafts a longer lease of life, and I only needed a bit of vein from your upper leg to complete the . . .'

'Re-plumbing,' I said.

He smiled. 'If you like. The internal structure of your heart was very sound so I was able to make good, solid grafts. You'll make a full recovery. In fact I think you'll feel a new surge of energy. You were quite fit apart from the damage to your heart. What sports d'you play?'

'I used to box and surf. Haven't done much lately. I walk a lot, play a bit of tennis. Go to the gym when I'm at home.'

'Keep it all up. It stood you in good stead. I see that you were in the military.'

'How do you know?'

'Wounds.'

'I got those mostly in civilian life. I was a private detective.'

He shook his well-groomed head. 'I can't think of a worse post-operative occupation.'

'I don't do it anymore. Aren't I a bit young for this? My check-ups were always OK.'

'It was almost certainly congenital. You must have had a propensity for a cholesterol accumulation to sneak up on you. Still, you're right. This sort of event often needs a trigger, other than the last physical effort you made. This is a research interest of mine. I believe emotional factors play a part. Have you had a major emotional upset in recent times?'

My lover, Lily Truscott, had been shot dead in Sydney five months before, shattering some dreams and half-formed plans. I'd played an unofficial part in the investigation

that led to the conviction of the killer. There was some satisfaction in that, but I'd stepped on a lot of toes and crossed
over some hard and fast police lines. There was no chance
I'd ever be licensed as a private investigator in New South
Wales again. You could say I'd taken two hard knocks—one
personal, one professional—and that wouldn't come
anywhere close to describing the emptiness I'd felt.

I'd come to the US to help Tony Truscott, Lily's brother,
prepare for a fight in Reno leading to the WBA welterweight boxing title. He won. I'd trained hard with Tony,
maybe overstretching myself. The loss of Lily was like a
constant ache so maybe Dr Pierce's research had something
to it, but I wasn't about to become one of his subjects.
Congenital would do me—I could blame my father. Put it
on the list of my other gripes against him.

'My father died in his fifties,' I said.

Dr Pierce looked disappointed but clicked his pen and
made a note. 'There you are.'

Megan arrived three days after the operation. She looks like
me—dark, tallish, beaky-nosed. She bustled into my room,
bent over and kissed me hard on both cheeks.

'Hi, Cliff. Sorry it took a while. Complications.'

'Good to see you, love. You said the right things when
it counted.'

'Shit, I couldn't believe it—Mr Fitness.'

'Not really, as it turned out. What complications? You
and Simon?'

It was spring in Sydney, fall in California. Megan had
dressed for somewhere in between, which was about right.
She ran her fingers through her hair, a mannerism she'd

inherited from her mother, before answering. 'Kaput. History. Not a problem.'

'I'm sorry. He seemed OK. You all right?'

'I'm better than all right. So, I saved your life, did I? That makes us even.'

I hadn't even known about Megan until my wife Cyn was dying and told me about her. Cyn was pregnant when we split and put the child out for adoption without telling me. Fair enough—back then I would've been the world's worst parent. Megan had tracked Cyn down when she was close to the end. She was keeping bad company and I took her clear of that. I hadn't exactly saved her life, but I'd stayed in her corner ever since. So we'd each been there for the other, and the feeling was good.

'The thing is, what's to be done with you? What's the drill?'

'They'll keep me hooked up like this for a while, they say, checking on the ticker and other things. Then they'll get me moving. A week at the most in the hospital and then out.'

'Jeez, that's quick. What'll you do then?'

'First thing—have a decent meal and a drink.'

'I'd have guessed that. Then what?'

'I don't think I'm supposed to fly for a bit. I like this place from what I've seen of it, and I have to stay in touch with the doctors and the physios for a while. How long can you stay?'

She shrugged. 'A week, I guess, ten days.'

Megan and I never pressed each other for details.

'Maybe you could line me up a furnished flat to rent for a month. Somewhere near the beach. Use it yourself to start with.'

I told her where my cash card was and the PIN. She gathered her bag and the discarded jacket and vest. 'I'll get right on it. Anything you want now?'

'A Sydney paper.'

I walked the corridors, did the exercises, took the medications.

Progressively, drains, canulas and the heart monitor were removed. They x-rayed and ultrasounded me and pronounced me fit to leave the hospital. I had leaflets on cardiac rehabilitation, diet and lifestyle choices. Appointments with the various medicos had been lined up. I thanked everyone who'd treated me. It cost eight hundred dollars to get out of the hospital—my meals and phone calls—but they assured me that the health insurance would take care of the rest. I'd resented paying the insurance for decades but now, not wanting to even think about what American surgeons and anaesthetists charged—I was grateful.

Megan picked me up in the car she'd hired. I wore the clothes I'd been wearing for my walk on the pier, the only difference being knee-length elastic stockings to combat the danger of post-operative blood clots. Outside, in the car park, I sucked in the first free-range, non-conditioned air in ten days. It had a touch of the sea in it as well as the ever-present American smell of petrol. My chest felt tight, my legs felt weak, my breathing felt shallow but I felt great. Megan stowed my bag and helped me into the car without any fuss.

She drove straight to a bar more or less attached to the marina. It had an outdoor area with tables shaded by umbrellas. The air was salty; surf beat on the sand; close your eyes, ignore the accents, and you could have been in a Manly beer garden. Megan ordered a pitcher of light beer.

'It's even more pissy than at home,' she said. 'But I thought you should start quietly. Would you believe I had to show ID to get a drink in here the other night? What's the legal drinking age—thirty?'

The beer came. I poured; we touched glasses. 'I think it's twenty-one,' I said. 'Be glad you don't look your age.'

'You look OK, Cliff. A bit pale.'

'I'll sit in the sun and clean my gun.'

'You're going to miss it, aren't you?'

The beer was thin and sweet but it still had enough bite to feel like a drink, a return to one of the great consolations of life. 'I suppose I will, but in a way this could be some sort of signal. Time for a change.'

'You've had a few of them—banned for life and . . . Lily.'

'Shit's like luck, someone told me. It comes in threes.'

Megan had found a first-floor serviced apartment in a small block on Newport Avenue in Ocean Beach. It cost a lot, but Lily had left half of everything she had to me. Her house in Greenwich was worth close to a million and she had some blue chip shares. Even after the lawyers and financial advisers had taken their bites, Tony and I were left comfortably fixed. I'd given Megan a substantial deposit on a flat in Newtown but left before I heard what she'd bought. Along with the money I inherited some guilt, because I'd never known that Lily had made that gesture.

'One floor up,' Megan said as she keyed in at the

security door. 'Gives you a bit of a view and you said they want you climbing stairs.'

'Right, and one flight sounds about enough just now.'

The flat had two bedrooms, a sitting room, bathroom and kitchen, all fitted out in US modern. There was a big fridge, a microwave, cable TV and DVD player and recorder. Sliding glass doors opened onto a balcony that gave me a view of the pier, the beach and the Pacific Ocean. That helped to make the price very reasonable.

'I stocked the fridge and the cupboards,' Megan said. 'You've got a month with an option to extend. How d'you like it?'

I put my arm around her broad shoulders and kissed the top of her head, which wasn't very far down. 'You done good,' I said.

'A woman comes in to clean every second day unless you put a notice on the door that you don't want it. All paid for.'

'I'll have to try and make it worth her while. Grot the place up a bit.'

Her look and tone were severe. 'Don't skite. The way you are, you couldn't make the bed.'

That's Megan.

They'd told me that I'd be exhausted on my day of release. I wasn't. We went out for lunch and then I was. I slept for a couple of hours and then went through the tedious process of the exercises. Arms up, deep breaths, rotate shoulders—again and again and again. And then it was on to the bloody nozzle and ball game—three balls inside plastic tubes. Suck to get them moving.

Megan laughed as she saw me struggle to hold the balls in suspension. On the third try I kept them up longer than I had in the hospital.

'Hey, that's pretty good.'
'I'm going to try out for the bypass Olympics.'

She stayed for three days—cooked me up some meals—
bolognese sauce, a couple of hot curries, a stroganov—and
froze them. I didn't ask her about the break-up with her
boyfriend, but she volunteered that she'd be moving into
the Newtown flat as soon as she got back. *Who with?*
I wanted to say but I didn't. Maybe no one, and she'd tell
me when she was ready. I thanked her too often, tried
to give her some money, which she refused, and saw
her off.

I settled into a regime of walks, exercises, more walks, more
exercises. At first I was slow, doing not much more than a
shuffle, but, as the physios had promised, improvement
came rapidly. After two weeks I discarded the elastic stockings and was walking pretty freely. I stayed on flat surfaces
for a while, then gradually tried myself on small inclines. In
the beginning I had to stand still to allow the ubiquitous
rollerbladers to avoid me, but eventually I was nimble
enough to avoid them. If there was a better place for rehabilitation than San Diego, I didn't know it. The temperature
hovered around the seventies in the day and there was a sea
breeze at night. It didn't rain.

I had some blood tests and reported to Dr Epstein who
expressed his satisfaction.

'You're making remarkable progress. Blood pressure
good, rhythm excellent, rate the same. Your heart is func-
tioning really well. Cholesterol's coming back into line.

You'll have to stay on the medications for the rest of your life. You realise that, don't you?'

'Doesn't worry me,' I said. 'Just to have a rest of my life's the bonus.'

'I'll refer you to a man in Sydney for you to stay in touch with.'

Dr Epstein put his hand on my chest and ordered me to cough.

'That sternum's solid,' he said. 'You can do pretty much anything you did before. You worked out, didn't you?'

'Yes. Nothing too solid.'

'Give it another couple of weeks and get back to it. You're going to feel ten years younger.'

So apparently I could get back to normal life. But what was that, with my career as a private enquiry agent effectively brought to a full stop? I put such thoughts on hold as I went about the rehabilitation full steam. Ocean Beach pier, the structure everyone is so proud of, is about a mile and a half long, taking in the main length and the two cross pieces—a perfect walking track with interesting things to look at along the way: the Vietnamese men and women, fishing for food, with their basic equipment; the others, for sport, with their high-tech rods and reels; the professionals in their high-powered boats. At the right times of day the bodysurfers were out and the windsurfers and the board riders.

It was the longest I'd ever stayed in one place in the US and I found it growing on me. Almost everything was commercialised, privatised, corporatised, except the people. They came in all shapes and sizes and colours and varied from aggressive semi-sociopaths to the utterly normal men and women you can find anywhere. Television was appalling, but books were cheap.

After a few days of walking the pier I had people to nod to—the guy from the bait shop, the professional photographer, other walkers. Then I met, or re-met, Margaret McKinley.

2

I was sitting on a bench near the end of the pier reading. Megan had left a pile of paperbacks she'd picked up and one was *The Power of the Dog* by Don Winslow. I was keen to read it because, in a way, Winslow had brought me to San Diego. His book, *The Winter of Frankie Machine*, was one of the best crime novels I'd ever read, and the description of the San Diego waterfront was so graphic and compelling I'd taken it into my head to go there as I slowly wended my way back up the west coast towards a flight to Australia. In the book, Frankie Machine ran the bait shop on the pier. The area had lived up to the description and it was lucky for me I'd been there when I had the heart attack. If I'd been driving around LA, as I was a few days before, things could have been very different.

'Hello, Mr Hardy.'

I looked up from the book. The woman standing in front of me was familiar, but I couldn't place her.'

'Nurse Margaret McKinley,' she said.

I half rose in the polite, meaningless way my generation was taught to do, but she put a hand on my shoulder to interrupt the movement.

'I'm sorry,' I said. 'I didn't recognise you out of uniform.'

'Understandable, a uniform's the best disguise there is, they say. May I sit down?'

I shuffled along, although there was plenty of room. 'Of course.'

'You look very well,' she said. 'I've seen you here before.'

'I walk the line,' I said.

She smiled, took the book and examined it. 'Ah, that explains it.'

'What?'

'What you said to Dr Pierce when you were coming to the surface. You said you were looking for Frankie Machine. We were puzzled. I see it's another title by this writer. I gather the book's set here.'

She was in her mid-thirties at a guess—medium sized with strong, squarish features and dark-brown hair in a no-nonsense style. She carried a sun hat and wore a white sleeveless blouse and denim pants that came to just below the knee; a light tan. Sandals. No ring. *Ah, Hardy, stripped of your licence, but still sizing up the citizens.*

'I don't think you were around when I left,' I said. 'I thanked everyone in sight.'

'I know. Everyone was very grateful. Your daughter came back and made a donation.'

'I didn't know that.'

'You're lucky to have her. I take it she's gone home?'

The way she said it made me pay attention to her voice. It was basically Californian but with an underlying tingle of something else. 'You're Australian,' I said.

'I was, still am at heart, but I'm a US citizen now by marriage. No hubby any longer, but a kid and a good job.'

I looked up at the clear blue sky and nodded. 'Living in climate heaven.'

She shook her head. Her face had the sort of lines that come from experiences good and bad but mostly good.

'Not really,' she said. 'Sometimes I yearn for Sydney's seasons. Even a bloody hailstorm.'

The Australian accent became slightly more pronounced with every word, the way it can when the other person is a genuine speaker.

'I suppose it might get you down over time,' I said, 'but just now it's perfect for my purposes.'

'I heard you say you were a private detective.'

'I was. I'm . . . retired.'

'You might still be able to help me. Could I buy you a cup of coffee?'

It was close to midday. 'What about a beer?' I said.

She had a nice smile. 'Why not, although it'd horrify my colleagues.'

We walked back towards the bar where Megan and I had sat and I told her about Megan's surprise at being asked for ID.

'Americans can be very funny about drinking. I know some who'd never dream of having a beer during the day or a glass of wine with their meals, but get bombed on cock-tails every night.'

'Unhealthy,' I said.

We sat at a shaded table and ordered two Coors, which a little experimentation had taught me was the beer closest to my taste. The frosted bottles and glasses came; we poured.

'To Sydney,' she said.

I nodded and drank the toast.

'When're you going back, Mr Hardy?'

'After all the services you performed I think you should call me Cliff.'

She laughed. 'You had trouble maintaining your dignity, didn't you? Perched on top of that bedpan.'

I'd been constipated for a few days after the operation and a proctologist had whacked in suppositories and let nature take its course.

'Made me feel human again, though. You said something about needing help.'

She told me that she'd left Australia fifteen years before to marry an American doctor who'd been holidaying in the wide brown land. The marriage hadn't worked out, but her Australian nursing credentials had served her well in America and she had no trouble getting work that allowed her time for her daughter.

'I was an only child and my mother died when I was ten. My dad was a geologist and his work took him all over the country. He did his very best for me, but I was often parked with people I didn't know and he was busy even when he was around. I want to be there for my kid a hundred per cent. Her father lives in LA. He visits now and then and contributes financially but not emotionally.'

For all the difficulties he'd had with his parenting role, Margaret said that she loved her father. She'd visited Australia twice during her daughter's holidays and he'd visited once. They corresponded by letter at first and electronically in recent times. Thirteen-year-old Lucinda valued the connection with someone she called her 'Ossie grandad'.

We were near the end of our drinks when she got to the heart of the matter. 'He's disappeared,' she said. 'I haven't heard from him for weeks and I can't find out anything about him. I email and phone the company he works for and get nothing useful. A couple of his friends say they haven't heard from him either. I'm very worried about him but I can't . . . I contacted the police and made a report but I've heard nothing back. I can't go home. I need this job, and Lucinda's involved in so many things that're important to her. I'm stuck.'

I asked some questions—like had he, Henry McKinley, been off on some up-bush expedition when she'd last heard from him. She said not, that he was city-based, working for a major corporation, about which she had few details. I asked about his age, his health and habits. She said he was fifty-eight, a cyclist, non-smoker and social drinker. As far as she knew he was wholly occupied with his work. His recreations were cycling, photography, archaeology and pen and ink drawing.

'He was . . . he is quite talented,' Margaret said. 'Lucinda seems to have some of the same knack. They swapped sketches over the internet.'

Saying that broke her composure somewhat and got through to me. I said I'd contact someone I knew in Sydney and try to get an investigation underway.

'I can pay,' Margaret said. 'Some.'

Amazing the freedom having money in the bank can give you. 'Don't worry about that,' I said. 'Let's see how far we can get.'

We talked some more. She gave me her email address and said she could provide documents, photos.

* * *

Getting fit, sitting in the sun, thinking about swimming, reading, watching HBO is all very well, but I knew I was going to miss my former profession and now I had that feeling for real, and very strongly.

Naturally the flat had a computer connected to the internet and a printer and scanner and other hardware unfamiliar to me. I'd kept my email address so as to stay in touch while I was overseas and I sent a message to Margaret McKinley to establish the contact.

I was never much of a web user but now I read some newspapers and blogs from home and was pleased to see that the conservative government was in trouble at the polls. The opposition was scoring better on most counts and the commentators were predicting a close election, with some reading it one way and some the other. I'd be back in time to cast my vote for change. It was well past time.

Margaret's message came through with a number of attachments—two photographs of Henry McKinley, one obviously taken a few years back showing him with his daughter and grand-daughter, who looked to be about ten. There was a photostat of his driver's licence and several newspaper clippings recording his winning a number of awards—one for a book on water management in the Sydney basin, another some kind of medal from the Australasian Geological Society, and one for the first over-55 finisher in the Sydney to Wollongong cycling race.

Margaret's notes said that her father owned the town-house he lived in at Rose Bay, that he had no pets and that his mail went to a post office box, so there was nothing at the flat to indicate that it was unoccupied. She included the phone number and URL of the corporation he worked for and documented the times she had made calls and emailed enquiring about her father. She listed the friends she had referred to when we spoke, and a number for the secretary of the Four Bays Cycling Club. It was an impressive dossier—she was obviously highly organised as well as very worried.

Henry McKinley was tall and lean with tightly curled fair hair. He wore wire-rimmed spectacles and his expression would best be described as good-humoured. Hard to judge from the snapshots and newspaper photos, but he looked weather-beaten, which I guess is natural for a geologist and a cyclist. He was born in Canberra, the son of a public servant father and an academic mother. He did his bachelor and master's degrees at the ANU, topped off with a PhD from Cambridge. He'd worked briefly as an academic but then branched out into consultancy, taking on commissions from state and local governments and the private sector. He'd worked for mining companies, presumably for big fees, and advised, *pro bono*, a couple of major archaeological excavations on the geology of their sites. In recent years he'd accepted a post as chief geologist in the Tarelton Explorations and Development Company.

I eased back from the screen after absorbing this information.

'A good bloke,' I said.

Spending too many days alone, I was beginning to talk to myself. It was definitely time to get in touch with other people. I phoned Margaret McKinley and told her I'd found the material she'd sent both helpful and worrying and that I was relaying it to a colleague in Australia with a recommendation that he begin an enquiry.

'Thanks, Cliff. Won't he need . . . what's it called? A retainer?'

'He'll need a contract, but we can deal with all that later. I'm booking a flight home for next week and I'll take it up with him then. His name's Hank Bachelor. He's an American, as it happens. Resident in Australia. The reverse of you.'

'Globalisation,' she said.

I laughed. 'Right. Can I see you before I head off?'

We met at a middle-range restaurant of her choice on the edge of the old town, walking distance from my flat. Margaret wore a dress, heels and a linen jacket; I wore a blazer, freshly dry-cleaned trousers and shirt, no tie. We'd dressed for what it was—somewhere between a date and a business meeting. That could have felt uncomfortable but it didn't. There was a confident easiness about her that communicated itself to me and we were soon chatting, ordering—oysters, fish, boiled potatoes and salad both— and enjoying ourselves. The place was busy without being packed and the service was casual but efficient. We had a bottle of Jacob's Creek chardonnay.

'We're going Dutch, aren't we?' she said.

I shook my head. 'This is my first meal in company since my heart attack. It's an occasion for me, and you're my guest.'

She smiled. 'Should've ordered caviar.'

'Not too late.'

'I've never liked caviar. Never saw what the fuss was about.'

I told her I'd relayed all the material she'd sent me to Hank Bachelor and that I'd see him about it as soon as I got back to Sydney.

'It's over a month,' she said. 'Doesn't look good, does it?'

'A month's not that long if he's had an accident and amnesia, or even if he had to take off suddenly for some godforsaken spot and can't get in touch.'

'Thanks, but . . .'

There was no point in kidding her and she seemed the type to be able to face facts. I asked her whether her father had made a will and she said she didn't know. I asked if he had life insurance or superannuation. She thought for a while.

'He said something once about managing his own fund. What are you getting at?'

'Just that if he's dead you'd be his heir, wouldn't you?'

'I suppose so.'

'We'll have to try to track down his lawyer. Maybe this Tarelton mob'll know.'

She went quiet and we got on with our eating and drinking. She'd already told me that she'd come by taxi because the San Diego police were red hot on DUI. She was drinking her share. I asked her a few things about her work but she barely answered. I tried to tell her something about the private enquiry game in Sydney but she scarcely listened. Eventually she put down her fork (she'd been eating in the American manner, cutting up the food and using her fork), without finishing.

'If he's dead,' she said, 'and if I inherit his house and his money, I'll come home to deal with it. But please, please, I don't want you to find that he's dead.'

And then she wept.

3

Tom Cruise in *Rain Man* was wrong about Qantas as he no doubt found out later when he was with Nicole—you didn't have to go to 'Mel-born' to catch it. You could pick it up in LA and fly to Sydney. I gave myself plenty of time to cope with the absurd security screening, tougher in my case because I had a couple of minor criminal convictions to my name. I'd pulled strings to get the entry visa, but the men and women, black and white, in the starched uniforms with the epaulettes checked and rechecked before conceding that Guantanomo wasn't an option. I travelled first class, stretching my legs, walking about to avoid DVT and enjoying the Australian accents, the beer and the barramundi.

'Been away long, Mr Hardy?' a steward named Frank asked, as he poured a Crownie.

'Felt longer than it really was,' I said.

'Right. Home in time to vote.'

'You bet.' I raised my glass. 'To better times and better people.'

A man sitting opposite heard me and did the same, repeating the toast a touch more loudly. I glanced around the section—more smiles than frowns. Encouraging.

* * *

At Mascot, I was met by Hank Bachelor and Megan. I shook hands with Hank, and resisted his attempt to take my cabin bag and my single suitcase. I hugged Megan.

She stepped back. 'We're an item,' she said. 'We think.'

I laughed. 'Since when?'

Hank said, 'We sort of got together when we heard about what happened to you in San Diego.'

Their happiness communicated itself directly to me and cut through the jet lag. 'I should be able to come up with something about the heart and growing fonder and all that,' I said, 'but I'm too knackered. Good luck to you. Let's have a drink.'

A few days later, installed back in my house and with outstanding correspondence and obligations, mostly financial but also social and medical, dealt with, I called on Hank in his Newtown office to talk over the Henry McKinley matter. I climbed the familiar stairs from King Street but now a fluorescent light made them more negotiable. As I was making my way up a man coming down fast bumped into me and almost knocked me off balance. He steadied me with a strong hand.

'Terribly sorry,' he said. 'Are you all right, sir?'

I was until you called me sir, I thought. I nodded and he went down, turning at the bottom of the stairs to look back. I signalled to him and went on.

Formerly mine, the office had been carpeted and painted and the windows cleaned. Hank had rented two adjoining rooms and put in partitions and doors so that he now had a small suite.

'You must be doing OK,' I said as I settled into a chair about three times more comfortable than the one I'd provided for my clients.

Hank shrugged. 'There's work about. The politicians and spin-doctors are worried about bugging, so I'm doing regular sweeps. Quick and easy and well paid.'

'Politicians on which side?'

'Hey, I'm a resident alien. I'm neutral. Both sides.'

'And you're finding what?'

'Paranoia and zilch, but who's complaining?'

'Any serious work?'

'Some insurance fraud—autos, personal accident. I cleaned up a couple of those cases you left me. Gave me a kick start.'

I'd seen another desk in one of the other rooms and one in a cubicle. 'You've got some help?'

He nodded. 'A casual. He just left. Must've passed you on the stairs. And . . . Megan.'

'How's that?'

'Cliff, she was keen. She's enrolled in the TAFE course. I got her associate status—provisionally.'

'What happened to acting?'

'She got tired of it, and it was going no place.'

My relationship with Megan was complex. Because I hadn't known her as a child, I didn't feel the full weight of a father's responsibility and attachment. I felt a lot of those emotions but not the full serve and, of course, I felt guilty about that. Complex. My warring feelings must have shown in my face and body language.

'She's basically a clerk,' Hank said.

'Stick around. She won't be for long. OK, we're all adults here. I'm not laying down any laws. How's the McKinley thing looking?'

Hank eased himself out of his chair the way a fit thirty year old can, took two steps and opened a filing cabinet. Forget the paperless office. Never happened. You can have anything you like on hard disk and flash drive but nothing beats a printed sheet when you want a quick grasp. Hank had several sheets in the standard manila folder and he spread them on the desk.

'Waiting for your input,' he said, shuffling the pages. 'I can tell you that there's something funny about this Tarelton company. Their website says they're a minerals and natural resources exploration company. You know that. But just where and what they're exploring and developing is kind of hard to pin down. It's a private company, so there's only so much it has to reveal about its personnel and operations and, in its case, that's virtually zero.'

'Margaret McKinley had the idea that it was paying her father well.'

'Oh, it's got assets—an impressive building in Surry Hills, staff, a fleet of cars. But what the hell does it *do*?'

'Who or what is Tarelton?'

Hank tapped one of the sheets. 'Edward Tarelton— South African or maybe Canadian. Fifty-one or forty-nine. Mystery man.'

'What happens when you make enquiries?'

'What the client said—the run-around. When I made a big enough asshole of myself that someone actually talked to me I asked about McKinley. Here's what I got.'

Hank flipped a switch on a console on his desk.

'We have personnel all over the world and do not discuss their whereabouts or assignments.'

'That's an illegal recording,' I said.

Hank shrugged. 'The machine was on, like, accidentally.'

'Who was that?'

'What's that expression you have? No names, no pack drill. What's that mean, anyway?'

'Take too long to explain. Well, we need to get busy—file a missing persons report with the police—'

'Did that.' Hank held up a card. 'Got a file reference.'

'—and a letter of authorisation from Margaret. I'll see to that.'

'Cliff, you're not a private eye any longer.'

'No, I'm a concerned friend, and I know a couple of cops who'll vouch for me.'

'And a couple of dozen who won't.'

'It's who you know, mate. It always has been.'

There's no law against talking to people or accessing public records. There were people who'd do me favours in return for things I'd done for them in the past, and others who'd have been pleased to hear that I'd dropped dead on Ocean Beach pier. The thing to do was make use of the former and avoid the latter. It's not even against the law to use a false name and claim to be something you're not, unless your intention is to defraud.

Margaret had given me a list of McKinley's friends with home and business telephone numbers—the secretary of the cycling club, Terry Dart, and the owner of a gallery where McKinley had exhibited some drawings, Marion Montifiore.

I had the names on a slip from the notepad that had come with the San Diego apartment. I got it out and was about to reach for the phone on Hank's desk when I remembered who and what I was. I covered the action by scribbling a meaningless note on the slip of paper before standing up.

'I'm going to follow a few things up, Hank,' I said. 'Thanks for what you've done. I'll make some copies of what you have in the file if that's okay, but I probably won't be bothering you with this.'

'I'm bothered already.'

'Come on—a geologist, cyclist, pen and ink man . . .'

'Working for a dodgy company.'

'Anything dodgy, you'll hear from me.'

I went home and phoned a supplier to get a new up-to-the-minute Mac computer with all the trimmings delivered by someone who could install it and teach me to fly it. That done, I had a light lunch, a rest as prescribed by the doctors, and then took a long walk around Glebe. My wind was good and I picked up the pace until I sweated.

I phoned the Montifiore Gallery, got the proprietor, and made an appointment to see her early in the evening. I drew a blank at both the home and business numbers for Terry Dart. I left voicemail messages at both numbers.

The gallery was in Harris Street, Ultimo, a walk away. I arrived at six pm as people were turning up for the opening of a new exhibition. The artists were a sculptor and painter whose names were unknown to me, which didn't mean anything—I couldn't name a single Australian sculptor alive or dead and very few live painters. The first challenge was the stairs—steep, concrete, two long flights. The other first-nighters were mostly young and handling the stairs easily. *Come on, Hardy*, I thought, *you can do it.*

I did, at a respectable pace, with only a little help from the rail on the last few steps.

The gallery was a large expanse, painted white with big windows letting in the last of the daylight and lights strategically placed to take over and flatter the exhibits. The crowd was a mixture of the affluent and the scruffy, possibly the scruffy trying to look affluent and the affluent trying to look scruffy. The paintings were abstracts that my eye skated over as though they weren't there; the sculptures were well-wrought wooden pieces—skeletons of boats, boldly carved figurines reminiscent of Nolan's Ned Kelly work and others difficult to interpret but interesting to look at. As the room filled, most attention focused on the sculptures and gave me the feeling that the red stickers would be coming out soon.

I made my way to the bar where a couple of kids barely old enough to drink were serving red and white wine. I accepted a glass of red for my heart's sake and asked if Marion Montifiore was present. One of the youngsters pointed to a fortyish woman with silver hair and dressed stylishly in black. She was talking animatedly about one of the paintings to a fat man in a suit who seemed more interested in her than the art work. That wasn't surprising. She was strikingly good looking with olive skin, dark eyes and features bordering on perfection. A matronly, overdressed woman led the fatty away and I approached before anyone else could nab her.

'Ms Montifiore? Cliff Hardy. We spoke on the phone this afternoon.'

It was one of those occasions when you like to present a card to obviate some explanations. It crossed my mind that I should get one—reading *Cliff Hardy* . . . and then what?

She turned her Tuscan eyes on me. 'Oh yes, about dear Henry McKinley.'

Her voice sounded as if it had been tuned to perfect pitch.

'I didn't realise it was an opening night. I'd have come at another time.'

'No, no, at these things you need all the bodies you can get. I saw you taking an interest in the sculptures. They're good, aren't they?'

'You saw . . .?'

She touched my non-drinking arm. 'I have eyes in the back of my head and at the sides. This is going quite well, I think. I can spare a few minutes. Come with me.'

I followed her through a door off to one side near the bar. The office was small, plain and furnished and equipped in impeccable taste. She sat on the corner of the teak desk; I stood. The chair on offer looked so comfortable I'd have been reluctant to leave it.

'I'm hoping you can tell me something about Henry McKinley,' I said.

That brought a frown. 'I don't understand. I thought you were going to be able to tell me . . .'

I shook my head. 'I'm sort of acting for his daughter who I met in America. She said she'd contacted you.'

'She did, but I told her I hadn't heard from Henry since his exhibition. I said I'd get in touch if I heard anything, but . . .' Her shrug was eloquent.

'Tell me about the exhibition.'

'Oh, it was a very small thing—four pen and ink artists with ten pieces each. I'd have to say that Henry's weren't the very best but someone obviously thought they were.'

'How's that?'

'Someone bought all ten. No, nine. One was slightly damaged and withdrawn at the last minute.'

'Who bought them?'

'I'm not sure I should—'

'Look, the man is missing. His daughter is worried sick and she's commissioned a private detective to investigate his disappearance. I'm working with that detective. I can give you a number to check on what I'm saying.'

I must have projected intensity, sincerity, something, because she suddenly looked concerned. The serene, beautiful mask cracked. 'He . . . he paid in cash. It wasn't a lot. Three hundred and fifty dollars for each. A little over three thousand dollars in all.'

'Carried them away under his arm?'

'Of course not. I tagged them and they stayed for the rest of the exhibition period. It was only ten days.'

'Then what?'

'Someone came to collect them, showing the receipt.'

'Is all that legal? What about GST, commissions, certificates?'

'It wasn't a lot of money and I knew Henry would be thrilled. Any artist would.'

'But he didn't get to see the red stickers.'

'No. I have to get back.'

'In a minute. I assume you took your commission. What is it—twenty per cent?'

'Forty.'

'Jesus. I'm in the wrong game. Describe the man and tell me about the drawings.'

I'd heard that people in the art business were tough and Marion Montifiore bore that out now. She moved off the desk and towards a cupboard. 'I haven't the least recollection of what he looked like. He was unremarkable. As for the drawings I don't have to describe them. I have the damaged one here. They were all much the same.'

She took something wrapped in brown paper from the cupboard.

'You can take it. You can tell Henry's daughter I have several hundred dollars held here which I suppose she can claim if . . .'

'Several hundred?'

'The total sale amount minus my commission and the rental fee the artists pay.' She thrust the package at me. 'Please go!'

The crowd had thinned out a little while we'd been talking. Fatty and his possessive partner had gone and there was almost no one taking an interest in the paintings. I was drawn back to the sculptures—particularly to the largest of the skeleton boats. The artist's name was Robert Hawkins and what he'd done to this beautiful piece of timber made you feel that something new and fine had come into the world under his hands. With Lily's money, I could have afforded to buy it, but I had nowhere to put it worthy of its quality.

I saw Marion Montifiore glaring at me from across the room, so I deliberately took my time examining the boat and other pieces. She could hardly order me to leave. I took out my cheque book, but all I did was scribble the artist's name down on the back of it. Petty, but she'd got under my skin. I didn't usually rub people up the wrong way as badly as I had her. Had to wonder if I was losing my touch.

4

I restrained my curiosity about the drawing until I got home. I'd left half of my red on Marion's desk, so I poured myself a glass and took a swig before tackling the wrapping. Her wine was better than mine, but she could afford it. Judging by what she said about her business, I wouldn't have been surprised if the artists had to pay for the opening.

I slid the drawing, on stiff, high-quality paper, out of its cardboard cylinder, unrolled it and spread it on the table, holding down the corners with books. I stared at the bold strokes, the white spaces and inked-in areas with total incomprehension at first. The more I looked the more certain associations formed. But they were very vague. I had the impression of something spacious, possibly circular and very much part of the physical world. An interpretation, perhaps an imaginative representation of something real. Or was I kidding myself?

Henry McKinley's signature appeared in small but clear letters near the bottom right hand corner, and the word 'North' appeared in slightly larger letters above it. *North? What did that mean?* I drank some more wine, usually an aid to thinking, but nothing else came to me. Marion Montifiore had said that the drawings were all similar, a set. So were the others South, East and West? And what else? North-east, North-west etc?

A crease ran from a few inches down on the left hand side to a few inches in at the top. It barely touched the drawing and was slight. I'd have been happy to smooth it out, shove the thing under glass and hope for the best. But then, I'm content with prints of the few pictures I like—a bit of Vincent, a bit of Brett, *Blue Poles*.

I thought it through as I finished the wine and set about making one of my three or four standard dishes— shepherd's pie. Obviously, the drawings meant something to the man who'd paid a fair amount of money for them. And he didn't buy them for their artistic merit because if he'd had an expert eye for the work he'd have noticed that the other artists had ten pieces on display and Henry only nine. *Where's the other one?* I'd have said. *And here's another two-fifty and bugger the damage.*

I needed access to Henry's house to see whether he'd left any information about the drawings. To be legitimate, that meant getting Hank to follow up the missing persons report and have the police enter the house. Legitimate, but not much use. There was no way the police would allow me to go in and, much as I trusted Hank's instincts in general, I needed to do the investigation myself. I needed to know whether my impressions of the drawing bore any relation to reality. I might come across drafts or notes. And if I stumbled across other things to do with Henry's employment, well, so much the better. There were ways to get into locked houses and I knew quite a few of them.

I put the drawing back into the cylinder and locked it

in a strongbox where I keep things like my passport, my birth certificate, divorce papers and the acknowledgement that I'd paid out the mortgage. I took the medication to control my cholesterol and thin my blood and went to bed. I thought I'd sleep well after the long walks but I didn't. The disappearance of Henry McKinley, the purchase of his drawings, the reticence shown by his employers had worked their way into me and I couldn't stop thinking about the usual questions—who, when, why, how? Those sorts of questions, with no answers coming through, can keep you awake.

I got up and settled into an armchair to read Julian Barnes's novel *Arthur and George*, and let the questions slip away as the old, empty house creaked and hummed around me.

I slept late. Went out for the paper and saw that the opposition was holding its lead over the government a week into the election campaign. I was absorbing this in satisfying detail and drinking coffee with more pills lined up, when the phone rang.

'Mr Hardy? This is Josephine Dart. You telephoned yesterday.'

'Yes, Mrs Dart. Thanks for calling. It's about Henry McKinley. I take it Terry Dart is your husband. I'm told he and McKinley are friends.'

I heard her draw in a breath and a change come over her voice. 'They *were* friends, very close friends. My husband was run down and killed by a hit and run driver when he was out cycling.'

'I'm very sorry. When did this happen?'

'A few weeks ago. Not long after Henry's daughter tele-phoned from America. Terry was very worried about Henry. I've heard of you, Mr Hardy. You were in the news earlier in the year, weren't you?'

'That's right.'

'You're a private investigator. Are you investigating Henry's disappearance?'

'Not officially, no. I'm . . . just looking into it for his daughter who I met in California. She gave me your number.'

'I want you to investigate Terry's death. It was murder, I'm sure of it.'

'I think we should talk,' I said.

Josephine Dart lived in Dover Heights in an apartment complex one block back from where the land drops abruptly down to the water. I had to check for the street in the directory, and I noticed that the Dart address was more or less directly in line with McKinley's address across the peninsula. Dover Heights isn't a busy part of Sydney. There are more apartments than houses, mostly with garages, so the streets aren't cluttered. No shops to speak of and no beach. The suburb gives the impression of having nothing to be busy about.

Apartments command high prices though, given the proximity to more exciting places, especially if a view is part of the deal. Good security. I was buzzed in and instructed to take the lift or the stairs. I'd chosen to walk from where I'd parked, mostly uphill, and I took the stairs to support my fitness regime. Standing outside the security door, I could see that the Darts had the whole package. The unit was three flights up and on the side of a building that was at the right angle to command a view south to Bondi, north towards Watson's Bay and east to New Zealand.

Josephine Dart was tiny, barely 150 centimetres in her high heels. She was perfectly groomed with a helmet of black hair, a pearl necklace and a blue silk dress. Her makeup was discreet, emphasising her large eyes and high cheekbones. She looked like a former ballerina, not that I'd ever met a ballerina, former or otherwise. Her voice was surprisingly strong, coming from such a small frame.

'Please come in, Mr Hardy. I've made coffee. I hope you drink coffee. So many people don't these days.'

The short passage gave onto a living room set up to be lived in. There was a leather couch, a couple of matching chairs, a coffee table, a magazine holder, TV and a sound system and bookshelves. None of it was excessively tidy: a few magazines drooped from the holder; there were loose CDs and DVDs sitting beside their racks; some of the books had been shelved flat. The room was dominated by two ceiling to floor windows leading out to a wide balcony. Some cloud had drifted over, muting the light, but the view could only be described as an eyeful.

'Sit down. I'll get the coffee.'

I prowled the bookshelves—an eclectic lot, in no particular order, ranging from sport to philosophy. Lance Armstrong's *It's Not About the Bike* sat next to *A Brief History of Time*. There was a strong showing of battered green and orange Penguins.

Mrs Dart returned with the coffee things on a tray. She pushed the morning paper aside on the coffee table and put the tray down.

She saw me inspecting the bookshelves.

'Terry was a great reader, from utter rubbish to quantum physics. I'm middlebrow, I'm afraid—biographies, memoirs and well-written thrillers. How do you take your coffee?'

I told her I took it black without sugar. She kept making inconsequential remarks as she poured and I judged that she was holding various emotions in—grief, anger, frustration. The coffee was excellent and I said so.

She sipped and nodded. 'Somebody killed my husband. I don't know why. We were childless. He was my life and I can't just let it go as if . . .'

She shook her head and drank some more coffee.

'I understand,' I said. 'You said your husband and Henry McKinley were close?'

'They were *very* close, like brothers. They shared . . .' She broke off and stared out of the window. The cloud had cleared and the view was stunning, but she wasn't seeing it. She was looking at something else, something inner. It was almost embarrassing to be present and I drank some coffee for protection.

'They shared almost everything—the same interests— geology, the outdoors, drawing, photography, cycling. I once said they ought to get a tandem bicycle and go riding on the one machine because they rode together so much. A sort of private joke . . .'

Geology, drawing, photography—was that a fatal connection?

I said, 'You'll have to tell me everything that happened.'

She left the room and came back with a folder containing a number of newspaper clippings. The tabloid and the broadsheet had reported on the death of Terence Dart, fifty-seven, of Dover Heights in a hit and run accident. Dart's body had been discovered at 6.05 am by a jogger on New South Head Road. He'd been thrown violently from his bike, which was a crushed ruin, and had died from massive injuries. Police called for anyone who might have been in the area when it happened to come forward. No one did, although there must have been light traffic at the time.

'I had Charles Morgan, my solicitor, press the police for details which they were very reluctant to reveal, but he did manage to learn that there were no skid marks, no signs of the vehicle swerving or losing control, even momentarily. Terry was deliberately killed.'

I sifted through the clippings. 'I think you're right. Did your husband wear a helmet?'

'He did, of course, always. But the autopsy showed that his injuries were to the neck and the upper part of the spine where the helmet offers no protection.'

She selected one of the clippings and pointed to a paragraph. 'The jogger said the bike was a ruin. Doesn't that suggest a terrific impact at a great speed?'

I nodded. It was clear what she was doing. Focusing on the forensic detail was helping her to keep grief at bay and herself together. She was going to make me part of that process and I was willing. I asked her about her husband's profession and the friendship with McKinley.

'Terry was a seismologist on a contract with the CSIRO. So of course he was interested in rock formations and the like. This wretched government had cut back on research funds so he was frustrated at being unable to pursue things as far as he would've liked. He said he was being phased out and had nothing to do but fill in forms and shuffle them. He and Henry argued about whether the private sector or the government sector held out the most promise. I couldn't follow the details, but I think they came to the conclusion that . . .'

'What?'

'That it really didn't matter. Government was in bed with business, business was in bed with government and science didn't matter a hang. Terry had some hopes that things might change, but . . .'

'Were they working together on anything? Informally maybe?'

She shrugged. 'Who can say? They rode their bikes for miles in all directions, further than I'd care to drive. They certainly . . . looked at things, took photos.'

'And Henry made drawings.'

'I suppose so. What are you getting at?'

I told her about the drawings and the mysterious buyer and the one that had slipped through the net. I said I'd show it to her to see if it gave her any ideas. That reassured her about my interest. I asked if I could look at her husband's workroom—his files, his photographs. She agreed. Then I popped the real question.

'And I need to do the same with Henry McKinley. Do you know who his lawyer is?'

'No. But that's not a problem, Mr Hardy. Not if you agree to follow this up for me.'

I nodded. 'As I said, I'm not officially engaged. I can look into whatever seems relevant.'

'I can pay you.'

'It's not an issue at this point, Mrs Dart.'

She looked up at me but it wasn't me she was seeing— it was something or someone else. I caught a flash of a sexual signal, quickly suppressed.

'Terry had a key to Henry's house. I have it right here.'

* * *

One of the rooms in the three-bedroom apartment served as Terry Dart's study. It was orderly, with a filing cabinet, bookcases, a laptop computer and printer and the usual jars with pencils and pens sticking out. I opened the filing cabinet, which was only sparsely filled with folders bearing names I didn't understand. Seismological terms. The books were mostly about that subject and related ones—vulcanicity, glaciation. He'd evidently read up a bit on global warming and alternative energy as well as the water crisis in Australia and elsewhere. The only personal touches were a set of trophies sitting on top of the bookcase.

Josephine Dart had sat in the room's easy chair while I made my inspection. 'Terry was very proud of those,' she said. 'He said they stood for aching muscles and gallons of sweat.'

Dart had evidently won a couple of long-distance road races and placed in a few more. 'He must've been good.'

'Good. Yes, when he was younger, but not at the top level. It didn't bother him. He was a lovely, calm, kind, considerate man from the day I met him until the morning he rode off. It's so bloody unfair.'

Something about the room bothered me. I opened the drawers in the desk—printer paper, cheque books, invoices, a postcode book, staples, printer cartridges, expended and new.

'What?' Mrs Dart said.

'Something's missing.'

She looked carefully. 'Everything's as he left it.'

It came to me in a flash. 'Where's his briefcase?'

She got up quickly. 'He kept it tucked down between the desk and the filing cabinet.'

The space, wide enough to hold a sizeable briefcase, was empty.

'Mrs Dart, have many people been in the flat since your husband died?'

She nodded. 'We had a wake . . . a party. My brother organised it. Terry was an only child. Terry would have liked it—they played some of his favourite music— "Bolero" and "The Ritual Fire Dance" and things from *Carmen*. There were quite a few people—neighbours and from the CSIRO and the cycling club. I didn't know them all.'

'Did anyone comment on McKinley not being there?'

'Of course,' she said sadly. 'It was a talking point.'

I asked her if she'd come with me when I inspected Henry McKinley's house but she refused.

'I went there quite often. Sometimes with Terry, sometimes without,' she said. 'We had some wonderful times together. I don't think I could bear to see it all empty and . . . dead.'

She produced five keys on a ring. I asked whether she wanted some kind of authorisation from McKinley's daughter or the private detective she'd hired.

'I thought you were the private detective.'

That was ticklish, but something I had to get used to. 'I'm more or less retired. I'm just doing this as a favour to Ms McKinley. She was a nurse in the hospital in California when I had a heart attack.'

'My goodness! You look fit now.'

'Yes, I'm fine.'

She gave me the keys. 'I trust you, Mr Hardy.'

You don't get a lot of that in this business and her remark buoyed me up even though I was sure there were things she wasn't telling me and that what I was learning added up to bad news for Margaret McKinley.

* * *

Henry McKinley's townhouse was part of a small set of newish places, modelled on the good old Victorian terrace. The architect had done his job well and the houses blended in nicely with the old and new stuff around them. The street was a bit back from New South Head Road and elevated, so that the houses had a view of the water with the trees of the Royal Sydney golf course off to the south. The security wasn't state of the art but it was adequate. A high, solid wooden gate at street level opened easily with one of the keys on the bunch and there was a security grille over the front door and bars on the windows on the lower level. A balcony ran along the width of the house and I could see greenery hanging down over the rail. The space in front was taken up with the traditional white pebbles and a few largish plants, looking bedraggled, in pots.

Another key opened the grille door and yet another the front door. I waited before going in. I hadn't been tentative about my approach, but I was prepared to defend it if challenged. No challenge came. The adjoining townhouses were quiet—professionals out earning enough to live there.

Light streamed in from a skylight halfway along the passage that led to a narrow set of stairs. I opened the door to the room immediately on the right. A bedroom. Double bed, neatly made up, the usual fittings, no sign of disturbance. Likewise the sitting room further down. The room suggested a non-fussy person of good taste. The furniture was comfortable rather than stylish. Neither the TV nor the sound system was new and the big, old bookcase with glass doors had the look of something handed down through the family—neither fashionable nor practical, but cherished. Its key stood in the lock. The books inside were a mixture of the very old—a Collins set of Shakespeare's plays—and the very new—Robert Hughes's autobiography. There was an emphasis on art and associated subjects—*Drawings* by Michael Fitzjames, *The Paintings of DH Lawrence*, a book on nineteenth century photography and three or four studies of Picasso.

The dining room was small but with space enough for a no-nonsense pine table and solid chairs; the kitchen had another skylight and about as much stuff as a single man would need to cook, refrigerate and sit down for a quiet drink. The wine rack held five bottles of red—five more than my ex-wife Cyn had left behind when we split. A door from the kitchen gave out onto a bricked courtyard where everything—flowers, shrubs and herbs—was overgrown. Bird droppings stained the garden setting; leaves had collected around the legs of the chairs and table.

A small aluminium shed occupied a corner of the court-yard. It was padlocked but a smaller key on the ring took care of that. A bicycle was held up on pegs attached to the wall. A heavy plastic cover was draped over it and there were tools I didn't recognise, cans of oil, jars of something or other arranged neatly on a shelf. Three helmets hung from one peg, three pairs of bike shoes from another. I felt sad about the well-cared-for things a man I didn't know had left behind him—if that's what had happened. I re-locked the shed.

I went up the stairs. There was a bathroom with a medium sized spa bath—something you'd need after those bike rides—a shower recess and toilet. At the back was a darkroom, fitted up with the red light, and the printing and developing equipment. The study was in the front. Both of these rooms had been searched, torn apart.

5

No help for it. I sent off a long email to Margaret McKinley bringing her up to date. Impossible to be optimistic. I told her that I'd located the name of her father's solicitor and his email address in my search of the townhouse, and asked her to contact him with an authorisation to talk to me.

My solicitor, Viv Garner, didn't think much of this when I told him what I was doing.

'I doubt he'll do it on the strength of an email,' he said. 'Give me the details and I'll get in touch and try to square it all away. Of course that's what you had in mind when you told me all this.'

'I'm an open book to you, Viv,' I said. I gave him the name. 'I want to get a look at McKinley's mail in his post office box. No way to tell if whoever searched the house found the key. Maybe he kept it on him.'

'That's very tricky,' Viv said. 'Takes time. You say she's hired Hank Bachelor to enquire into her father's disappearance. You're involved, of course, but you've got no status with the police or McKinley's lawyer or his employer.'

'Moral authority,' I said, and I told him about Josephine Dart.

'Moral authority's not worth shit. But you'll do what you want to do, I know that. I'll try to smooth out some of the snags. Who do I bill for my time and effort?'

I grinned. 'Who else but Hank?'

I calculated the time difference and rang Margaret McKinley.

'Emails can be a bit cold,' I said. 'I wanted to talk to you and answer any questions. And see how you're holding up.'

'Thank you, Cliff. It's funny, it's all so far away but just hearing you makes it seem a lot closer.'

'Is that better or worse?'

'I'm not sure. You say the police and the lawyer are the next people to approach. What about Dad's employer?'

'I think we need to know as much as we can about the circumstances before tackling them. Our initial approaches, like yours, haven't got anywhere.'

'I was so sorry to hear about Mr Dart. I know how fond Dad was of him.'

'Like brothers, his wife said.'

'What do you make of her?'

I realised that I hadn't formed a clear opinion. 'I suppose you'd say she was vibrant, also sad and angry. She wants to hire us to look into her husband's death . . . which she's sure was murder. She could be right.'

'Would that be a conflict of interest?'

No way to dodge the question. 'Not if the two matters are related.'

'You think my father's dead, too, don't you?'

'Margaret, I think the best hope is that he found he was in danger of some serious kind and has gone into hiding.'

'That doesn't sound like Dad.'

I thought, but didn't say: *Or that someone is holding him to force him to do something.*

She picked up on the pause. 'God, I know it looks bad, but I'm still hoping.'

'It's all speculation. I'll tackle the lawyer. Hank will give you his email address and you should alert him to what we're doing. Depending on how that works out, we'll gee up the police and the media to get busy.'

'This is all going to cost a lot of money. I can raise—'

'You're not to worry about that. I can cover the cost for now and we can sort things out later, depending on the results.'

'Why would you do that?'

'For selfish reasons, mainly.'

'I don't follow.'

'I'll explain another time. Meanwhile, please just do what you've been doing—authorising things and people— it's all you can do for now. Oh, I'll get Hank to scan this drawing of your father's I mentioned and send it. See if it means anything to you. How's the weather?'

'Like always. Thank you, Cliff.'

I rang off. She was a smart woman and the explanation for why I was putting in the time and the kilometres wouldn't have been hard for her to grasp—I was grateful to her for providing me with a chance to do the sort of thing I'd done for more than twenty years. It was work I enjoyed, mostly, and which I'd done well, mostly. I hadn't come up with any ideas on how to occupy myself for the rest of my life, which, according to the medicos, was a good long stretch if I looked after myself. Certain avenues were blocked and others—golf, monitoring my investments, hobby farming—didn't appeal. For now, I didn't have to think about it. Selfish, as I said, and not something you want to parade with a loved, missing father at the centre of things.

I emailed the bits and pieces of information I'd collected so far to Hank.

Horace Greenacre had an office, or rather a suite of offices, in Double Bay, above the boutiques and bijou shops of various kinds. It was accessed through a heavy glass door at street level with his name etched on it and a deep-carpeted staircase. Over the years I'd had a few clients in the suburb and, despite their money and/or their pretensions, their problems turned out to be much the same as people's everywhere—deceit, greed, love, hate. But solicitors there are more specialised than those in less affluent areas. They tend to deal in family trusts, quiet transfers of assets and the briefing of QCs when their clients get into trouble—which they do.

Viv Garner had smoothed my path, so I was ushered into Greenacre's office by his secretary with more deference than I'd encountered in lawyers' precincts in the past. Strangely, being an 'associate' of a licensed PEA and a client and friend of another member of the legal profession earned me more respect than being a private detective myself.

Greenacre was in his fifties, impeccably groomed and suited with a trim figure that suggested gym membership and diet tonic with his gin. Although Viv must have told him about my being drummed out of the profession,

Greenacre didn't let on. He got up from behind his desk to greet me a few steps inside the door and shook my hand.

'Mr Hardy, I'm very glad to meet you. I've been worried about Henry for some time. Can't reach him. Come in, come in and let's talk. Viv Garner has a very high regard for you and of course I'll help in any way I can. Have a seat.'

He went behind his desk but slid his chair partly out so that it wasn't a complete barrier between us as I took a chair off to one side.

'Mr Greenacre, I'll be blunt—'

'Horace.'

An old trick, always works—interrupt the flow, allow a second to size a person up. 'Horace, are you telling me you've had no communication from Henry McKinley for nearly two months and have no idea where he is?'

Greenacre wasn't fazed, or not much. He picked up a sheet from his desk, looked it over and put it down. 'I resent the implication but I appreciate the need to ask the question. The answer is no.'

'Thank you.'

'I've had a communication from Margaret McKinley, several in fact. Again, singing your praises. She asks, authorises you might say, me to answer any questions you might have. I'm prepared to do that, up to a point. Fire away.'

'In his last meeting with you, whenever that was, did McKinley express any concerns, doubts about the work he was doing, worry about his personal safety?'

'No.'

'Were you involved in the contractual arrangements he made with Tarelton Explorations?'

'Henry showed me the contract. The remuneration was handsome and the undertakings the company made to provide research facilities and staff seemed generous. I thought some of the restrictions were severe—limitations on what could be published and a long period after the expiry of the contract whereby Henry couldn't do much of anything at all. The sort of thing leftists want to impose on former government ministers and the like, but Henry said he was happy with the arrangements and I saw no reason to advise him otherwise.'

'The contract was to run for . . .?'

'Five years.'

'That seems a long time.'

Greenacre shrugged. 'They evidently valued his contribution.'

'Do you know anything about what that might have been?'

'No. The details of Henry's professional work are way beyond me.'

'Me too. Last question. McKinley's will. Any strange bequests? Anything surprising?'

Now he displayed some professional caution. 'What are you getting at?'

'The man's disappeared. There are signs of some sort of . . . disturbance in his affairs. Let's face it, he could be dead. I need to know if his will reflects anything unusual in his past, especially the recent past.'

'I thought you'd ask that and I checked the will. This is tricky. I certainly can't go into details while Henry's whereabouts are unknown.'

'I'm not asking for details.'

He took up another sheet of paper. 'Printout of Ms McKinley's email,' he said as he reread it. 'Just making sure I understand her instructions precisely.'

I wondered what she'd written, not that I was ever likely to know. This man played strictly by the book. He put the sheet down and shook his head.

'There's nothing unusual in the will. Just exactly what you'd expect.'

'I assume Dr McKinley had investments?'

'Substantial.'

'Who handles his financial affairs?'

He shook his head. 'Before answering that I'd need further instruction.'

I thanked him and left Hank's card asking him to get in touch if any information came his way. Horace didn't like me one little bit, but he wanted to keep Margaret McKinley as a client in the hope of doing business with her. To that end he was prepared to be polite to me. Just.

My car was still up on blocks in a friend's garage awaiting a final service and tune-up, and I'd caught a cab to Double Bay. I hadn't been away more than six months but Sydney traffic seemed to have got worse, if that was possible. It was stop, start and crawl for long stretches and the new tunnels didn't seem to have had any good effect. On the return trip, glad I wasn't driving myself, I had plenty of time to think about the next move. Two options—get the police on the job or tackle Tarelton Explorations directly.

I'd put it to Hank. Might have to persuade him a little, but I was pretty sure which way he'd jump. The taxi dropped me in Newtown and I went up the steps to Hank's office under the newly installed fluorescent light. In my time there, you could scarcely see your hand in front of your face on that stairway. Hank wasn't the only tenant to have upgraded his premises. The way things were going, the landlord would be stressing them all by raising the rent.

Hank was on the phone in one room and Megan was on the internet in the other. Both looked up, made welcoming signs and got on with what they were doing. *Kick your heels, Hardy. You're supernumerary now.*

Megan got free first and I asked her what she was doing.

'Confidential,' she said.

'Jesus!'

She stood and kissed my cheek. 'Hello, Cliff, are you feeling as well as you look?'

'You'll get on. Yes, love, I'm fine. Back to my best at the gym.'

'Really?'

'Well—nearly. I'm here about the McKinley matter. How busy is Hank?'

'Busy enough, but he'll find the time. The coffee maker's more or less where you had it.'

She went back to the computer. I wanted to ask her how things were going between her and Hank but I didn't: our relationship didn't quite reach into those personal zones. Not yet, maybe never. I had to be content with what I had and, mostly, I was. I watched her out of the corner of my eye as I made coffee, and saw myself in her olive complexion and dark hair. There was something of her mother, though, in her powers of concentration and her cool manner. Cyn could work me over with that attitude whenever she chose, and she did.

'Hey, Cliff!'

Hank advanced towards me—all 195 centimetres and one hundred kilos of him.

'Hank,' I said. 'What've you done to the coffee? Smells drinkable.'

'Blame Meg.'

Meg is it now? I thought, but I said, 'I want to move ahead on McKinley.'

Hank beckoned me into his office.

'I'm with you on this, Cliff. I know it's important to you, but—'

'I'm paying.'

'Say again.'

'As of now, you're on a full retainer and expenses. I'll arrange an account debit and . . . however the hell these things are handled now on an ongoing basis.'

Hank leaned back in his chair and studied me as I sipped the coffee. 'You sure about this?'

'Look—we've got a missing man whose study and darkroom have been searched to the point of destruction, his close friend, possibly murdered, whose briefcase was stolen. Coincidence? I don't think so. You've got an anonymous person buying up the missing man's drawings and an employer not cooperating. Plus . . .'

'Plus what?'

I told him about my interview with Josephine Dart and my feeling that there was more to her connection with McKinley, and maybe more to McKinley himself, than met the eye. I said I'd talked to McKinley's lawyer, who would play along for a certain distance.

'This is a workable case,' I said.

'Sure it is. But throw in an ex-private eye working the street and financing the investigation himself, that puts a spin on it.'

There was no point in trying to put one over Hank. He

looked like a jock and often talked like a jock, but he was smart and a good reader of people. I finished the coffee and put the cup on the desk.

'OK, you've nailed me. I'm attracted to the woman and I need something to do. Is that good enough for you?'

I surprised myself with the first part of the statement and the sincerity I'd expressed. That did the job for Hank. He clapped his big hands together. 'You lay it on the line, man. What d'you suggest?'

'A direct approach to the Tarelton people.'

'Tried it once, remember. Got fobbed off by some dude in personnel.'

'Do it again, mate. But this time get across that you've learned McKinley's home has been broken into and searched, that his closest friend has had a fatal accident and that a possibly significant McKinley drawing is in your possession. Tell the personnel bloke to get that message through to the higher-ups.'

'Will do,' Hank said.

6

I went to the gym in the morning—treadmill at a moderate speed and gradient, free weights and the machines. What I'd told Megan was true; I was almost back to what I'd been doing before. I told myself I'd reach precisely that level next session. Something had been holding me back and I wasn't sure what. I didn't like the feeling of unconscious caution, if that's what it was.

I had a massage from Wesley Scott, the manager of the gym and a longstanding friend.

'You healed good,' Wes said, looking at my scar which was now just a slightly discoloured line running down the middle of my chest. The hair that had been shaved off was growing back. Pretty soon the scar would be all but invisible.

'Purity of mind and body.'

Wes snorted. 'Lost some muscle tone along the way. Getting it back, I'd say. Not quite there. Take it easy, Cliff. Don't push it. Remember, man, you were dead but for a computer and a little old electric machine.'

'Thank you so much, Wesley,' I said. 'Just rub, will you?'

* * *

Hank rang to say that he had an appointment with the head of personnel at Tarelton for that afternoon.

'I want to come along,' I said. 'You can do all the talking. I just want to look and listen.'

Hank's hesitation was momentary. 'OK. Make a copy of that drawing and bring it along. Might help.'

'That's a very good idea.'

The Tarelton building was on Elizabeth Street, a few blocks from Prince Alfred Park—named after a royal back in Victorian times. I don't remember that he ever did anything useful. Not many of them did from that day to this. Tarelton Explorations was housed in a three-storey building painted a becoming shade of grey and renovated to within an inch of its life. It had probably been a red brick factory or warehouse, but now it featured tinted windows, big sliding glass doors and a marble-floored lobby with glass cases displaying models of some of the projects the company claimed to have participated in—a dam, a bridge over a river, a tunnel under a river and a lake that doubled as a decoration for a beach resort and a wetland for wildlife. I couldn't figure where exploration came into it, but it did occur to me that the lobby would be a good setting for Robert Hawkins's boats.

Hank and I were a little early and we studied the models with interest.

'Pretty green oriented, this stuff,' Hank said. 'I'm seeing that everywhere these days.'

'Hadn't noticed,' I said. 'Tell you what though, with

these lights and the air conditioning, the building's laying down a fair carbon fingerprint.'

'Footprint, Cliff, footprint. Time to go.'

We checked in at a high-tech reception desk, were given security passes, and took the lift to the second level. A good-looking woman in a suit and blouse that stopped just short of being a uniform met us and we were escorted down a corridor. Discreet lighting through the tinted glass, framed blueprints on the wall, a rock garden with fountain at a bend.

She opened a door with 'Personnel' on a nameplate and nodded to the man and the woman working at computer desks. She knocked on a door that carried the name Ashley Guy.

'Come,' a voice within said.

I glanced at Hank, who was fighting off a grin.

She opened the door and waved us in.

Ashley Guy was sitting behind a big desk studying a printed sheet. He stood when we came in and held out a hand to shake. We shook. He sat down and gestured towards two chairs. The room was spick and span, as if some brain work might go on there, but nothing as mundane as filing or keyboarding or signing things. Guy wore the unbuttoned waistcoat of a three-piece suit with a light blue shirt and dark blue tie. He looked to be in his mid-thirties, with his fair hair thinning and his waistline thickening.

'I can't give you a lot of time, Mr Bachelor and Mr . . .?'

'Clifford,' I said.

'. . . Mr Clifford, but I'll do whatever I can to help in the time available. Of course, we're very concerned about Henry.'

'Likewise his daughter, likewise the police pretty soon,' Hank said. 'Our enquiries have turned up grounds for more than just concern, but I thought to come to you before bringing in the police with . . . all guns blazing, as you might say.'

'These grounds are . . .?'

Hank shrugged. 'Kind of circumstantial, but it'd help a whole lot if you could tell us precisely what Henry McKinley was working on.'

Guy shook his head. 'That's precisely what I *cannot* do. That information falls under the heading of commercial confidentiality. Every research project here involves us in the outlay of a great deal of money, sometimes for no return. Competition in our field is intense. Perhaps you understand, being in the business you're in.'

'Maybe I do,' Hank said, playing him a little.

Guy hesitated, glancing uncertainly left and right, before taking a slim file from a desk drawer. 'Anything else—his medical record, qualifications, references, salary, in general terms, contractual provisions, in outline—I'll be happy to give you.'

'Healthy, was he?' Hank said.

'Very.'

'Solvent?'

'Yes.'

'With time to run on his contract?'

Guy wasn't stupid. 'You know this already, don't you?'

'That's confidential,' Hank said. He nodded to me. I took a folded-up high quality photocopy of McKinley's drawing and put it on the desk.

'Someone,' Hank said, 'don't know who just at present but we're working on it, missed this when he bought up a whole set of McKinley's drawings. This is a copy, naturally. Mean anything to you, Mr Guy?'

Some say watch the eyes, others watch the mouth; some say look for a frown or hand movements. I know you'd be flat out doing all those things at once and a good liar probably didn't show anything. Guy looked closely at the drawing, moved it a little, and then shook his head.

'It appears to be well-executed to my inexpert eye, but I'm afraid I have no idea what it means.'

'We're in the same boat,' Hank said, 'but it certainly means something because someone paid out quite a few hundred dollars to gather up the ones that went with it.'

Guy shrugged. 'You've got me. Was there anything more?'

Hank stood up and I followed suit. 'Is there anything more, Mr Clifford?' he said.

I took the drawing and folded it. 'I'd say there's a good deal more, but that'll do for now.'

Hank executed a courtly half-bow, the way Americans do. 'Thank you for your time, sir.'

We went out quickly. In the corridor we could see our escort hurrying towards us but Hank held up his hand, shook his head and she stopped.

'We're fine. Sure you've got better things to do.'

The woman looked nonplussed, but we were on the move and to trot after us wouldn't be her style. We strolled down the corridor, studying the blueprints as if they meant something to us. When we reached the waiting area for the lifts I touched Hank's shoulder.

'Got your mobile?'

'Sure.'

'Snap a picture of that bloke there waiting for the up.'

Hank did it with the speed and secrecy I'd known he'd be capable of. We rode the lift to the lobby, handed in our passes, and left the building.

'Thirsty work,' I said. 'Must be a pub around here somewhere.'

We found one in Elizabeth Street and settled down over middies of Old.

'He wasn't a personnel man,' Hank said. 'Someone higher up.'

I nodded. We'd both noticed the same things: the 'Ashley Guy' nameplate had been slid in on top of another but not exactly, so that a centimetre of the previous one still showed, and Guy's uncertainty about which side of the desk the drawers were on when he reached for the file.

'Means they're worried,' I said.

'Plus, I never trust a man wearing a three-piece suit.'

Hank took out his mobile and studied the photograph. The man was big, florid, overweight, in an expensive suit and with an expensive haircut. 'Who is he?'

'I don't know, but he's familiar. It'll come to me.'

Hank took a long drink and sighed. 'That's real beer. Are you cool about me and Megan, Cliff?'

'You've both been around long enough and had enough experience to know what you're doing. I hope you're good for each other. I'd say the chances are better than even.'

'I should've known not to expect a straight answer.'

'There aren't any straight answers to real questions.'

Back in the Newtown office, Hank plugged the phone into one of his computers and printed out the photograph. He laid the print on his desk and the three of us gathered round to look at it.

'Likes his lunch and dinner,' Hank said.

Megan looked at us both. 'You really don't know, do you?'

I said, 'I feel I should, but . . .'

'That's Hugh Richards,' she said, 'shadow minister for minerals and energy in the state parliament.'

'I'm a bit out of touch,' I said. 'How solid's this state government?'

'They're on the nose,' Megan said. 'You must have seen the stuff in the papers—law and order, transport, water . . .'

'I thought that was standard state politics—shit on the last lot while they try to shit on you. And nothing gets done except calls and hand-wringing over the things people want to do—like gambling, watching porn, drinking and taking drugs.'

'Jesus,' Hank said. 'That's fundamental cynicism.'

'He's right,' Megan said, 'but it looks a bit worse for this government. The word is there's a high profile child sex abuse case with a drag component coming up and some DUI matters that could be very embarrassing.'

'How d'you know all this?' I said.

Hank mimed clattering a keyboard. 'She reads blogs.'

'I'll have to try to find out what that means, exactly,' I said. 'What about this Hugh Richards?'

'The things that're protecting this government,' Megan said, 'are four-year terms and the useless opposition. But Richards is thought to be a possible saviour. I'll do some work on him.'

7

Hank had arranged a Skype hook-up with Margaret McKinley so that we could all see each other on the computer screens. It was late at night for us, early in the morning for her, but that was fine because she was due to start an early shift. She was in her nurse's uniform, looking crisp and competent.

'Hi, guys,' Margaret said. 'You've been busy. Don't worry. I know there's no good news. I've adjusted to that.'

She'd had emails from Hank and me. She held the faxed copy of her father's drawing so we could see it. It had lost some of its definition in the transmission but still had a powerful clarity of line and shading.

'The original's better, Margaret,' I said, 'and we're keeping it safe for you. What d'you make of it?'

'Hello, Cliff. I'll be glad to have it. I haven't got a lot of Dad's stuff. He was a perfectionist and he didn't keep what he didn't think was up to scratch. And he sold a bit, so thanks. I've looked at it from every which way, and the only thing I can come up with is—a quarry.'

Hank and I looked at each other.

'That's a whole lot better than anything we thought of, Ms McKinley,' Hank said. 'A quarry. Why not? Facing north, or looking north, or something.'

The admiration in Hank's voice brought a smile to Margaret's face, animating it. She was an attractive woman with the attraction usually muted by her concerns and responsibilities. Now it showed through to its best advantage.

'Will that help?' Margaret said.

I gave her a positive nod, wanting to do more. 'It could. It really could.'

'Gotta be lotsa quarries around,' Hank said after the hook-up finished.

'I dunno, probably not that many these days. They tend to be used as landfill or get topped up and turned into parks. I don't like the feel of it though, if Margaret's right.'

'Holes in the ground, you mean?'

'Yeah.'

'She seemed like a pretty together woman. I'd say she could handle whatever comes up.'

I nodded. 'I think so, too. Hardest thing would be not ever knowing.'

Hank yawned. He was putting in long days working a couple of cases. 'Suppose it was the Tarelton crew who bought the drawings and the drawings are of a quarry, so what? What d'you find at the bottom of a quarry? Rocks?'

'Or water,' I said.

'I'll get Meg onto a quarry search. Ain't nothin' she can't do with Google. She tells me she's digging up all she can on this Hugh Richards.'

Tired as he was, Hank was still on the job. He shuffled through what he had in the McKinley file. 'Shit!'

'What?' I said.

'Margaret says he drove a Toyota SUV. Spare tyres, spare gas, he could go any place.'

'It wasn't meant to be easy.'

'Hey, I've heard that. Who said it?'

'A former prime minister. Used to be a villain, less of a villain these days.'

'What do you think about the guy you've got in now?'

'Beyond redemption.'

I drove home and took my medications with water and waited a while before I made myself a nightcap. Hank would be going back to be with Megan. Good luck to them. I made the drink a strong one. Loneliness wrapped around me like a sweaty sheet on a hot night. I thought of Margaret McKinley in her white uniform with her dark hair held back by a red band. I finished the drink and took the image up to bed with me with the Barnes book. The book was still good but the image didn't do me any good. I had a restless night.

Stefan Gunnarson had been a senior officer in the Missing Persons Division for a good part of my career as a PEA. We'd got on well in a rough and ready way, and I was glad when he'd got the top job. We hadn't had any dealings after that but when I learned that his son, Martin, was now in the spot with the rank of inspector, I was encouraged to ring Gunnarson senior, who'd retired, and ask him to put in a word for me with the head man. Stefan Gunnarson was one of those cops who'd still have a drink with me after my licence was cancelled. He said he'd talk to his son and that was how I came to be sitting in Martin Gunnarson's office in the Surry Hills Police Centre securing a small slice of his time. I'd emailed him a rundown on the case.

He was a duplicate of his dad—short, heavy set, dark, nothing like your stereotypical Scandinavian.

'This is all highly irregular, Mr Hardy,' he said, fingering a slim file in front of him.

'It's not only regularity that gets results. Ask any proctologist.'

He winced. 'Dad warned me about your jokes.'

'That's the only one, I promise. You'll admit it looks very dodgy—no sign of him or his car, house broken into, strange goings on about his drawings . . .'

'Agreed, but the trail's very cold.'

'The daughter posted him missing weeks back and Hank Bachelor followed up a while later.'

'We're understaffed and stressed.'

'So you outsourced it to the private sector?'

Gunnarson didn't say anything. He didn't have to. The defiant set of his heavy features said it all.

'Look,' I said, 'I don't want to get on the wrong side of you. I'd like you to do the usual thing—print some flyers, talk to the media.'

'Why do I have the feeling there's something more?'

'And bring some pressure to bear on Tarelton Explorations. They're . . . involved.'

'They're also influential.'

'That right? All the more reason. I'm just suggesting you have someone senior pay a call, ask a few questions.'

'And you'll do what?'

'See if feathers fly.'

'We can't act as your . . . what d'you call those servants that go out to scare up the pheasants for the nobs to shoot at?'

'Beaters.'

'Right, beaters.'

'Your dad did just that, a couple of times, and he didn't regret it.'

'Are you saying he owes you and so I owe you?'

'No. I messed things up once big-time and we're square.'

Gunnarson laughed. 'How have you stayed alive so long?'

'I sometimes ask myself that.'

'I bet you do. I'll send someone and you'll get an edited report.'

'Edited?'

'I've bent over, but I'm not going to let you fuck me.'

Megan had been very busy. She was compiling a list of quarries in an area stretching from Nowra in the south to Newcastle in the north and west to the Blue Mountains. She refused to tell me how many she had so far and I didn't press her. I was more interested in what she'd turned up about Hugh Richards.

'He's a nasty bit of work,' she said. 'A God-botherer, as you'd expect given the party he belongs to. Very narrowly escaped prosecution for tax evasion and fraud back before he got into parliament. He's rich, with interests in a string of companies, all that at arm's length now, of course.'

'Of course.'

'The word is that he's still actively involved in some of those companies and that he's a busy share trader.'

'How does he get away with that?'

'There's a theory, and I got this from your mate Harry Tickener, that he's got something on the bosses in his party and maybe on one or two in the government.'

'Great. Just what we need, a political angle.'

Nothing happened for almost a week as Megan kept googling. I went to the gym, took my meds, checked that a flyer about McKinley was posted on the web and in the usual places, and that reports about his disappearance appeared in the press. Nothing on TV. Then Hank got a call.

'From Chief Superintendent Ian Dickersen of Serious Crimes,' Hank said. 'He wants me and you and any materials we have on McKinley to come in to Surry Hills this afternoon. I guess I'm free. You?'

'Yes. Any more information?'

'About zip, except that I think he mentioned the word conference, and I gather your pal Gunnarson's going to be there.'

'I wonder if we should take a lawyer with us?'

Hank tapped his mobile. 'I've got my guy briefed and ready to spring into action.'

We rolled up at the appropriate time and were escorted to a conference room with a large table and comfortable chairs—for a police station, that is.

Dickersen was forty-plus, polished, part of the new breed. Not scruffy, not flash, not fat, not thin—a man for all occasions. He introduced himself, introduced Gunnarson to Hank and introduced the woman present, Detective Sergeant Angela Roberts, to both of us. She was black, part of an even newer breed.

When we were seated Dickersen said, 'DS Roberts interviewed a person named Guy at Tarelton Explorations. I thought it might be useful for you to compare notes with her.'

Hank and I nodded in her direction. They'd have to be mental notes—neither of us had brought a single sheet of paper. If Dickersen noticed he didn't comment.

'Well, to business,' he said. 'We've found Henry McKinley. I'm sorry to have to tell you that he's dead. He appears to have died violently.'

It wasn't unexpected, but you always hold out hope. It'd hit Margaret hard.

'That's not all,' Dickersen said. 'I understand you and McKinley's daughter are close, Mr Hardy.'

'In a way,' I said.

'We'll leave it up to you then whether to tell her the rest or not.'

'That is?'

'Seems he was held for some time—ligature marks.'

'Tortured?'

'Possibly, hard to say.'

8

Henry McKinley's body had been found near a fire trail in the Royal National Park. An attempt had been made to torch his car but it had been only partly successful, and the condition of the body allowed the pathologist to make several conclusions. McKinley had died of cardiac arrest. There were ligature marks on his wrists and ankles and bruises to his chest and legs.

'The . . . injuries were extensive,' Dickersen said, 'but the pathologist said his heart was dodgy—a couple of blockages. It's possible the beating, or a number of beatings, could have triggered the heart attack. Or just stress from the . . . circumstances he was in. He'd been gagged. I'd be stressed, from the sound of it.'

There was an eerie quiet in the room as Dickersen went into the details. When you hear of a thing like that you can't help mentally putting yourself in the victim's place and feeling the chill of fear—me particularly, after my recent experience. You don't say anything; you just wait for the feeling to pass.

Gunnarson broke the silence. 'Some firemen found the car and got straight onto the police. Luckily, no media came to hear of it and we kept it that way.'

I said, 'You're sure it was McKinley?'

'Everything the pathologist documented about the body fitted the description the daughter gave us and the more detailed one that Mr Bachelor provided.'

Hank said, 'I didn't tell you, Cliff. Our client said that her father had broken his right arm and his left shoulder in different falls from his bike.'

'That checked out,' Gunnarson said. 'We found that McKinley was a blood donor. His DNA's on record and that's being matched, but I don't think there's any doubt.'

Hank took a notebook from his pocket. 'When was the body found?'

Gunnarson looked at his watch. 'Close to seventy-two hours ago.'

'And how long since he was killed?'

'Not long. That rainstorm we had last Friday probably contributed to dousing the fire.'

I felt the weight of that. McKinley was alive when our investigation began. Another thing that'd be hard to convey to Margaret, but that wasn't my only problem.

'I have to ask,' I said, 'why are you giving us all this pro-tected information? And, with respect, why is DS Roberts here?'

Dickersen tapped the file in front of him. 'Mr Bachelor and you have the inside track on this matter. As an apparent case of murder this is particularly serious in its . . . execu-tion. We've decided that we have an advantage in keeping it under wraps. We assume the perpetrators expect us to find the body and for the media to go to town on it. When that doesn't happen they may become anxious.'

Hank said, 'You're going to keep an eye on the spot in case someone comes to check?'

'That, too, but we want your cooperation in giving us every scrap of information you have and maintaining the security blanket.'

Hank glanced at me. 'I'd say we could guarantee that, Chief Super, but, again with respect, as you say, how good is *your* security?'

'Very good,' Dickersen said.

Hank nodded. 'But not absolute.'

Dickersen shrugged. 'What is?'

This was new territory for Hank and me—total co-operation with the police. The same question occurred to us both—was this sharing of information mutual? Hank asked for a few minutes for us to confer and we went into a huddle at the far end of the table while the police did the same at their end. We mapped out a strategy.

When we reassembled, I said, 'You spoke of us inform-ing our client of her father's death. That'd be a breach of this security, wouldn't it?'

'We'd ask you to withhold the information for a time while the investigation proceeds.'

'That'd be deception on our part and would cost her money,' Hank said.

'Some measure of compensation might be possible.'

'That's very vague,' I said. 'Tell you what, we do have some additional information that could be relevant, and we'll share it with you.'

'Good,' Dickersen said.

'On the condition that a question we have is answered. That is, that DS Roberts tells us where she fits in and we decide we're happy with her explanation.'

At a nod from Dickersen, she took a notebook from her pocket and cleared her throat. I gave her an encouraging smile, which she ignored. 'At Inspector Gunnarson's direction, I interviewed the assistant to the CEO at Tarelton Explorations—a Ms Barbara Guy. The CEO, Edward Tarelton, AO, is out of the country on business, allegedly. Ms Guy gave me copies of a whole bunch of documents relating to Henry McKinley's employment, but refused to tell me anything about his area of research or what field investigations he might have done.

'I asked if Dr McKinley had had a secretary or an assistant I could interview and she said he hadn't. I asked who was closest to him in the firm and she said he was a very private person who had no close in-house relationships, as far as she knew. I asked to see his office and was told it had been reassigned and that all his files were covered by commercial confidentiality.'

'A fun interview,' Hank said.

She relaxed a little—Hank can have that effect. 'At first, it was like hitting a ball against a brick wall. Then she tried to pump me about what we knew about Dr McKinley's . . .' she consulted her notes, '. . . absence, she called it. My turn to play a dead bat.'

Hank said, 'A dead bat?'

'Cricket term,' I said. 'I'll explain later.'

'My report to the inspector suggests that Tarelton Explorations is sensitive and evasive about Henry McKinley. Outwardly cooperative, but actually very obstructionist. I believe they have something to hide and should be regarded as of interest in the investigation of Dr McKinley's murder.'

Paul Keating said something like, 'We'll never get this place set up properly until we find a way to get everything settled with the Aborigines.' He was right on the grand scale and on the personal level as well. DS Roberts's statement was a model of clarity and judgement and I wanted to say so and would have normally, but how patronising would that look? We haven't found that way yet. Everyone around the table nodded.

Gunnarson said, 'Thank you, Angela. I hope that satisfies you, Hardy.'

'It does,' I said. I risked the patronisation trap by adding, 'And for my money, I hope DS Roberts can stay on the investigation team.'

'So?' Dickersen said.

After getting the nod from Hank I told them about Terry Dart's death and the theft of his briefcase. I had the copy of Henry McKinley's drawing in my pocket. I unfolded it and filled them in on the attempt to suppress the set.

'Three thousand dollars isn't a lot of money,' I said, 'but it isn't chicken feed either. I got the impression from the gallery owner that the buyer would have paid, whatever the asking price.'

'Find that buyer and you've got a fair way into this thing,' Hank said.

All three had been making notes. Gunnarson looked up. 'Is there a good description of the buyer?'

I shook my head. 'Worse than useless.'

'We're not in good shape,' Dickersen said. 'We can keep the surveillance on the car for a few days but we can't keep the whole thing under wraps for much longer. McKinley's daughter has to be told and we'll have to appeal for witnesses who might have seen activity in the park. The media'll take a pretty keen interest, at least for a while. As I see it, we don't have leads, just a suspicion about the Tarelton company. DS Roberts is going to interview the CEO when he gets back and see how he reacts to this news about one of his employees. Something might come of that.'

'Like what?' Hank said.

Dickersen shrugged. 'Maybe McKinley was caught up in something that went wrong. Who knows? Could be industrial espionage. Maybe Tarelton has a rival, an enemy of some kind. Might give us another line of enquiry. But that's about it at this stage. Wouldn't you agree?'

Hank and I exchanged looks and we both nodded.

Dickersen said, 'I propose that we liaise through DS Roberts. Share whatever information comes our way.'

'That was weird,' Hank said on our way back to Newtown. 'Never said a word about you being on board, unlicensed and all.'

'It was odd all right,' I said. 'They're playing a very cagey game. I don't imagine for one minute that they told us everything, do you?'

Hank shook his head.

'Which was why we didn't tell them Margaret's guess about the drawing.'

'Yeah, but Dickersen's right—no real leads to follow.'

'We've got the quarries and they're bound to have something. It's interesting.'

We were in the train we'd caught at Museum—the best way to get around the city and our part of the inner west. There were only three other people in the compartment, all Asian and, as it turned out, all bound for Central and then Newtown. Two looked like students and the other, middle-aged, groomed, in a thousand-dollar suit, looked as if he might own a sizeable chunk of King Street. He spoke in a low voice on his mobile the whole time, switching easily from an Asian language to English and French.

We were walking south along King Street when my mobile rang. I listened and broke into a run.

'What?' Hank said as he loped along beside me.

I stumbled, fought for balance. 'Megan. She's been attacked.'

9

It was the first time I'd broken into a full run since the heart business. Hank, with youth and a longer stride on his side, passed me easily but I more or less kept up with him except on the stairs, which he took three at a time. We found Megan sitting on a chair in her office with her feet on a stool being fussed over by Grant, the gay podiatrist who occupies rooms on the same level. Simultaneously, I saw the blood on the towel she was holding to her head and smelt the powerful fumes of petrol.

Hank rushed up to her, almost pushing Grant aside. She let him take the towel away to reveal a long cut on her forehead that had obviously gushed blood and was now still flowing. Hank put the towel back. Megan's expression was alert. She showed no signs of shock, plenty of anger. She didn't exactly shoo Hank away but she clearly didn't want to be comforted. I stood where I was.

'What happened?' I said.

'Megan . . .' Grant began, but she waved at him to be quiet.

'I got back from buying coffee to find this fucker backing out of our space, sloshing petrol around. I threw the coffees at him and tried to kick him in the balls. He hit me with the petrol can. I got in one kick before I dropped. He fell down the stairs. I hope he broke his bloody neck.'

'He didn't, love,' I said, 'but you did pretty good.'

Grant said, 'You macho types. Time to call the police.'

Hank had picked up on Megan's attitude and abandoned the solicitude. He eased Grant towards the passage.

'We'll take it from here,' he said. 'Might need a statement. Did you see this guy?'

Grant shook his head. 'What're you going to do about the petrol?'

'Be careful with matches,' Hank said.

'Petrol and blood,' Megan said, 'an exciting combination.'

'Oh, God,' Grant said, 'quotations.'

I took a closer look at Megan's wound. 'It needs stitches. Better get you up to RPA. I'll do it, Hank, and then take her home.'

Hank hesitated, but Megan reached for his hand, gave it a squeeze, and nodded.

I heard Grant say, 'Someone has to get on to cleaners, carpet people and the insurance company.'

I helped Megan down the stairs and we got a taxi to the hospital. An open, bleeding wound gets quick treatment and she was cleaned up and stitched and given a tetanus shot and some painkillers all inside an hour. She insisted she could walk back to her flat.

'You helped me buy it,' she said. 'Time you took a look at it.'

The flat was in a narrow street two blocks south and one or two west from King Street, part of an old warehouse that had been gutted and done over. It was on the second level, had two bedrooms and a balcony looking out onto Camperdown Memorial Rest Park. The décor, furniture and everything else displayed Megan's taste—plain, functional, unfussy.

'Hank keeps his own flat by mutual agreement,' Megan said. 'Bit like you and Lily did. We divide our time between the two places.'

'It can work. How're you feeling?'

'Okay. I'm going to have a drink and take a couple of these pills and then I'll feel better until I bomb out. What'll you have?'

'Same as you.'

We sat on the balcony—minimal traffic, nice breeze over the park, gins and tonic.

Megan touched her forehead. 'Honourable wound, professional hazard. Bet you took a few.'

'I still might, the way things are going. Any regrets about . . . getting involved?'

Megan washed pills down with a solid slug of her drink. 'Thinking about it.'

'Good. Tell me, love, does Hank have anything on his plate that'd bring this on—an attempt to wipe out his whole operation?'

She was fading fast but she made an effort to concentrate. 'There *is* another arson matter involved—torching Dr McKinley's car—but this isn't the same style. I can't think of anything else. It looks like the McKinley case.'

'Hank's not exactly going to thank me for bringing it to him.'

She smiled. 'He thanks you for *me*. That'll cover it.'

Hank phoned and said he'd be with her in an hour. He was going to lock the office up and pay a couple of local kids he'd used in the past to run messages, to keep an eye on the building overnight.

'Reckon we should tell the cops?' he asked.

'Let's not,' I said. 'Let's think about it. See if there's some way we can make it work for us. I'm tired of stumbling around in the dark on this thing.'

I left Megan lying on her bed with her eyes closed. The G & T had been solid and the analgesics had kicked in. Hank wasn't likely to get any conversation from her until breakfast time.

I was halfway down Australia Street heading back to Glebe, a bit tired but walking briskly, when a car pulled up beside me. Two men got out. I recognised one of them—Detective Senior Sergeant Phil Fitzwilliam of the City Command Unit. An old enemy, Fitz had avoided corruption charges by the skin of his teeth several times. As a young copper he'd been decorated for bravery and in his early years as a detective he'd made some significant arrests and secured some notable convictions. That reputation had sustained him in later years when he sailed close to the wind. We'd run up against each other several times, never pleasantly.

'Hello, Fitz. How's tricks?'

Fitzwilliam had been a lean six-footer in his prime, but beer and big dinners had inflated him and he'd lost centimetres as if he'd had to stoop to carry the weight. His pale blue eyes were sunk in creased, sagging fat.

'You were always a smartarse, Hardy. That's what they'll say at your funeral. I heard you nearly booked in for one. Pity it didn't happen.'

'From the look of you, I'd bet on me going to yours rather than the other way around. Not that I would.'

Fitz turned to the other man. 'See what I mean, Detective Constable? Always with a comeback. Never at a loss for words, but an arsehole just the same.'

His colleague nodded sycophantically. At a guess he was thirty, twenty years younger than Fitz, and with a lot to learn.

Fitz turned his bulk slowly and pointed to their car. 'Come on, Hardy. We've got things to talk about.'

I wasn't really worried. The old days, when cops like the famous 'Bumper' Farrell, and imitators like Phil Fitzwilliam, would take you somewhere quiet and beat you so the marks didn't show, were gone. Physical intimidation was out of fashion, but there were plenty of other methods. Also, Fitzwilliam had a very uncertain temper—provoke him too much and he just might react violently. I felt fit and strong, but a broken sternum is a broken sternum and I didn't want to be on the end of one of Fitzwilliam's wild swings.

I sat in the back of the car with Fitzwilliam while the young policeman drove. For some time Fitz said nothing, which was unlike him. He enjoyed the sound of his own voice, boasting, exercising his authority. I tried to look unconcerned and to keep quiet while the driver did a skilful U-turn and headed back towards Newtown.

'Do you remember being scrubbed as a private detective by the Board? For life?'

'I do.'

'It's come to my attention that you're making enquiries as if that ruling meant nothing to you.'

'It's not quite—'

'I don't give a fuck what it's not quite like. Your mate Bachelor is allowed to employ associates as long as they have the appropriate qualifications. You bloody well don't and you know it. Bachelor's licence is hanging by a thread.'

He was right. The PEA's Act is specific on this matter and rightly so. Can't have people running around doing the job without the training.

'Make your point, Fitz.'

We were travelling down King Street and the driver made the turn into Missenden Road, cut across to Bridge Road and headed towards Glebe. Fitzwilliam said nothing until we pulled up in front of my house.

'There you are, Hardy. Brought you home. Don't say I never did nothink for you. And I see you've spent some money on the joint.'

I had. Front garden cleaned up, guttering replaced, tiles and pavers expertly relaid, fence and gate renewed and painted. All done while I was away.

'A tidy-up,' I said, reaching for the door handle.

Fitzwilliam grabbed my arm; pudgy though he was, he still had a strong grip. 'I haven't forgotten the couple of times you put me in the shit, Hardy. You and that mate of yours—that fuckin' Parker. I don't like you. I don't like you inheriting money from your dead slut of a girlfriend, and I don't like you surviving a heart attack and coming up roses.'

I wanted to hit him, but you just can't do it. 'I'd feel the same about you if things were reversed.'

'I can't do bugger all about all that—nothink, but I can tell you if you go on playing fuckin' private eye, I'll get Bachelor's licence lifted and I'll find a way to get charges laid on you both. Piss off!'

He released me, opened the door and used his bulk to shove me out. The door slammed and the car drove away.

Interesting development. Would Phil Fitzwilliam have the clout to get Hank's licence lifted? I doubted it. So far Hank had a pretty clean sheet and it takes more than one infringement to bring about a cancellation. I should know; I had a pile of them before I finally went too far. There was no question that Fitz hated my guts and wanted to get even with me, but it was an odd way of going about it. How had Fitz heard about our investigation of Henry McKinley's disappearance? There were several ways—a leak from the Missing Persons Division, information from Josephine Dart, or a spin-off from Hank's enquiries. The last was the most likely and that brought the Tarelton company squarely into the picture.

I didn't go in for interior renovation of the house. I liked it the way it was, and with some new carpet, fixing of the staircase and some quarry tiles to replace the kitchen lino, I was content. I'd had a bit of rising damp treated, a few walls repainted. On the advice of the people installing wireless broadband and Foxtel I'd spent money on the wiring. The insurance company would be happy about that.

Not wanting to mix my drinks, I sat in the breakfast nook in the kitchen with a gin and tonic on the scarred table and thought about Fitz. Among those in the know, he'd been notorious for taking kickbacks from companies and individuals for information about police interest in their affairs. With ICAC and other watchdogs active, he'd probably gone quiet on that lately. But, since the Tarelton enterprise, with headquarters in Surry Hills, was firmly inside Fitz's patch, could it be that he was on the payroll?

I missed Lily. In recent years, with cases like these, I'd formed the habit of laying the evidence, or, lacking any, the assumptions and theories, out for her and getting her opinion. More often than not she'd come up with a useful suggestion that would clear the fog and suggest a course of action. But the fog was thick now.

I tried to remember when I'd last eaten and couldn't. I was losing weight from all the walking and skipping meals. I made myself a sandwich and ate it although I had no appetite. The ache for Lily; the attack on Hank's office and the damage to Megan; the threat from Fitzwilliam and the nagging feeling of lifelong dependence on medications were nagging at me. I wondered if I was still up for this kind of work, even as a supernumerary. Then the phone rang.

10

'Cliff, it's the middle of the night and I woke up with a bad feeling. Has something happened?'

I don't believe in the paranormal, but this sort of thing occurs. It's just a heightened anxiety in my book. You don't hear about the times the alarm proves to be false.

'Yes, Margaret, your father's body has been found. He was killed. I'm very sorry.'

A pause, and then her voice shook. 'I've tried to prepare myself for it. I've seen lots of deaths. But you can't, can you, when it's your own people?'

'Not really, no,' I said. 'If you need some time now you can hang up and call back. I'll be here . . .'

'No! I'd rather have you there. I mean I'd rather be with you. Oh God, I'm confused. Just talk to me about it.'

'The police are involved and cooperating with Hank and me. We're doing everything we can to try to find out who did it. For the moment it's under wraps.'

'Why?'

I explained about the police strategy.

'Will that work?'

'I doubt it, but it's worth a try. The story'll have to get

out soon because the police'll be asking for witnesses and they'll want media coverage, but for now . . .'

'How did it happen?'

'It seems that he died from heart failure, but he'd been attacked and injured.'

'He was a strong man, I bet he fought back.'

'Nothing of this is public knowledge. Don't say anything to anyone. Not even to Lucinda.'

'I understand. Cliff, I'll have to come home, won't I?'

'You will. Can you arrange it?'

'I've got some leave accumulated and Lucinda's been agitating to see her father and her new half-sister. Her holidays are coming up. She can stay with them. I can swing it. Take a few days.'

'Do that,' I said, 'and text me the details. I'll meet you and you can stay here. I've got a spare room. Nothing fancy.'

'I don't need fancy. I need someone to talk to and for . . . answers and explanations. My poor dad . . . he didn't deserve anything like this.'

No answer to that. We talked briefly and then she cut the call. I told her she could ring any time and I sat by the phone with the dregs of my drink for a while thinking she might press for more information but she didn't call back.

I rang Megan's number early the next morning and got Hank, as I expected.

'How is she?'

'Up and about, Cliff. I tried to tell her to take it easy but she wouldn't listen.'

'Her mother was that way.'

'And like you're not? She's gone to Victoria Park to swim laps, and she says as soon as I do something about the gas—

sorry, petrol—in the office, she'll get on with the quarry research. Says she's come to like quarries. They have interesting histories. Wants to buy one.'

Margaret McKinley was the sort of person who did what she said she was going to do. They're not all that thick on the ground. I'd got my car back and I met her at Mascot three days later in the evening. She looked tired and strained but also exhilarated. Generally speaking, Sydney isn't a bad place to fly into—not too hot, not too cold and you can mostly count on a clear sky. That's how it was and she was appreciating it.

She gave me a sort of hug, which I returned. Casually dressed in slacks, a blouse and a loose jacket, she'd travelled light, with just her cabin bag and a medium-sized suitcase. We trooped through to the car park and she stopped me after I'd opened the boot.

'Let me have a look at you.'

I put her case in the boot and turned and stood for her inspection, selfconsciously.

She nodded. 'You've completely recovered, haven't you? More energy than before the heart alarm? Taking better care of yourself?'

'Right,' I said.

'I knew you'd come good.' She laughed. 'Listen to me, I'm talking Australian already.'

'A couple of days and you won't be able to tell the difference. It's great to see you, Margaret. I'm just sorry it's not under better circumstances.'

'I've known in my heart of hearts for a while that he was gone. That he didn't embezzle a million dollars and take off to South America, or have a fall and be in an amnesiac fog somewhere.'

No remote. I opened the passenger door with the key. She smiled at the old-fashioned operation but didn't say anything. I got in and started the engine.

'I had to tell Lucinda her grandfather had died. I didn't give her any details.'

'Sure. The media have the facts now and they're covering it. Some of the facts, that is. I've got the papers at home and a record of one of the TV reports.'

'Some of the facts?'

I was out in the traffic, coping with the aggression of the cabbies and the competitiveness of some of the other drivers. I swore as one cut in front of me. I felt her touch my arm.

'Sorry,' she said. 'Just drive. Plenty of time to talk.'

She was wearing shoes with a small heel. She eased them off and leaned back in her seat. She'd obviously freshened up before landing. I could smell some kind of perfume, very faintly. She ran her fingers through her hair, shook it out, and the action had an immediately erotic effect on me so that I had to grip the wheel and concentrate on my driving more than was needed.

'I guess this isn't the scenic route,' she said as we travelled through streets crammed with transport warehouses.

'There isn't one. They made some improvements for the Olympics. But you've been back since then, you said.'

'Once only. Dad collected us and took us straight up to a resort on the central coast. Bliss. And straight back. I scarcely saw Sydney.'

'Lots of changes,' I said. 'Bridges, tunnels, toll roads, e-tags, half a million plus for a single-storey terrace in Newtown.'

'Jesus. As students we rented them for next to nothing. What else?'

'Starbucks, Gloria Jean's, more Maccas.'

'Tell me something good.'

'Lots of Asians, Africans, Middle Easterners, mostly getting along, and a bad government looking as if it's on the way out.'

'Fingers crossed,' she said. 'There was a piece on that in the *New York Times*. I've been trying to catch up.'

It was dark when we got to Glebe and my house always looks a bit better in the dark—more gracious and imposing than it really is. We went in and I showed her the upstairs spare room with its three-quarter bed, wardrobe and table with the new computer and accessories.

'Bathroom's next door, and there's one downstairs.'

'Thanks. Nice room, nice house. Very you, Cliff.'

'Meaning?'

She laughed. 'Haven't seen a three-quarter bed in a while.'

'It's to deter couples from staying too long. Get yourself set and we'll have a drink. Gin? Scotch?'

'Gin with plenty of tonic, or I'll be on my ear.'

'Something to eat?'

'I ate on the plane. It reminded me of that joke about the plane crash, where the survivors ate the bodies of the dead and then the on-board meals.'

She was holding up very well, but I had to wonder how she'd feel when she saw the familiar sights in daylight, and went to her father's place, saw his bike, the original of the drawing. I had the drinks ready when she came down. She still looked tired but less tense. I settled her into a chair and we touched glasses.

'To Henry McKinley,' she said. 'And screw the bastards who killed him.'

We drank the toast.

'I'm buggered,' she said. 'That's a bloody long flight in economy. In the morning you can tell me more of those facts you've held back.'

I nodded. She finished the drink and then did what I do—ate the lemon slice. She got up and kissed me, not on the mouth but close.

'Don't be alarmed if I'm up at three am with advanced jet lag.'

'There's a radio in the room and the TV and CD player down here. Tea and coffee making in the kitchen. I'll set them up for you. Just pretend you're in the Hilton.'

'I'd rather be here.'

She went up the stairs. A floorboard creaked on the landing. I remembered how it always creaked in just that way when Lily trod on it. There was a photo of Lily on a shelf not far from where we'd been sitting. If Margaret had seen it she hadn't reacted. I looked at it now and felt the ache.

I hadn't eaten since the morning and I suddenly felt the need for fuel. I microwaved some leftover curry and freshened my drink. I ate and then set out the tea and coffee for Margaret and made sure the mugs in the drying tray were clean and that the milk in the fridge hadn't gone off. Sugar on the bench, bread in the basket near the toaster.

I sat in the living room that still carried a trace of Margaret's presence in the air and tried to free-associate about the McKinley case. After a while I decided that I didn't know enough about Henry McKinley. Was anyone that pure? That dedicated? That uncomplicated? Not in my experience. From what I knew so far, it sounded as if he had no life apart from work, cycling and a long-distance relationship with his daughter and grandchild. I didn't believe it.

I needed to know more about the texture of his life in Sydney. Does a fit, healthy, well-heeled widower lead a celibate life? I didn't think so. Someone must know something closer to the bone. Josephine Dart? Moving on from that, I needed to know more, a lot more, about what kind of work he was doing for the Tarelton mob. They'd closed the doors pretty tight, but there's always an opening somewhere. A weak link. Ashley Guy?

I fished out my notebook and scribbled these things down. Sometimes this stuff, done late at night with drink on board, turns out to be froth and bubble in the morning. Sometimes not.

I took my late-night meds and went up to bed. No light showed under the spare room door. I'd finished the Barnes novel, tried another of his books without success, and started on *Port Mungo* by Patrick McGrath—about an artist who was a bit of an arsehole, like some I've known. I read about half before quitting and turning off the light.

Lines from Adam Lindsay Gordon buzzed in my head as I drifted off:

> *Life is mostly froth and bubble,*
> *Two things stand like stone.*
> *Kindness in another's trouble,*
> *Courage in your own.*

Bit banal maybe, but his bust is in Westminster Abbey. Les Murray'd never make that.

11

If Margaret had a disturbed night I didn't know about it. I woke up from a sound sleep to the smell of coffee. I found her in the kitchen in white silk pyjamas and a kimono-style dressing gown, pressing the plunger.

'Morning, Cliff. That bed's okay. I slept just fine. Coffee?'

'You bet.'

'Toast?'

'No, thanks. Orange juice with my bloody pills and coffee and that's it.'

'I'm ravenous.'

She put two slices of bread into the toaster and poured the coffee.

'I could do you scrambled eggs,' I said. 'I remember how from my cholesterol days.'

She laughed. 'Maybe another time. Who's the woman in the photo, if you don't mind me asking?'

I didn't. 'Lily Truscott. We were together for nearly five years. She was murdered. That's one of the reasons I took off for the US.'

She studied me for a moment, then nodded and dealt

with her toast. We were sitting across from each other in the breakfast nook.

'You wear a preoccupied look now and then. Would that be about her?'

'Sometimes it would. Sometimes about Megan; sometimes, quite often, about myself. And about your father . . . and you.'

'Tell me now what you haven't told me.'

I gave it to her straight—the dumped and burnt car, the signs of her father having been held over time, the possibility of torture of some kind, maybe triggering the fatal heart attack. She took it well. Probably the nurse training helped, but there was something else working in her, holding her together. When I finished she reached across the table and touched my hand.

'Thanks for telling it like it is, Cliff. I hate being patronised . . . protected. I'll see Dad's lawyer and find out exactly what's coming my way. Probably a lot, and you know what? My first priority is to find out who killed him. Mr Bachelor and you . . . you'll stay on it, won't you?'

'We will, but . . .'

'I know, no guarantees.'

I told her about the attack on Hank's office and how, thematically, that tied in with the burning of her father's car but otherwise didn't point solidly in any direction. Likewise, the securing of the drawings. I didn't mention the approach from Phil Fitzwilliam—given Fitz's corrupt history that could tie in almost anywhere.

'Is Megan okay?' she said.

'Swimming laps the very next day.'

'I'm looking forward to meeting her again.'

* * *

Margaret showered, dressed pretty much as she had the day before with a fresh blouse, and I drove her to Newtown. She sent her daughter another text message on the way. She'd seen the house, now she saw the office in all its austerity. She could have no illusions about the size of the operation. Didn't faze her. The carpet had been replaced and the petrol smell was faint. The door to the office, previously always kept open, was closed and a peephole had been installed.

'How do the others feel about what happened?' I asked.

Megan smiled. 'I'm the heroine of the hour. They're just glad the whole joint didn't go up in flames.'

Margaret was businesslike with Hank, friendly with Megan. She used the phone to arrange a hire car and called for a taxi to take her to the depot. I'd given her a key to the house.

'See you back there,' she said, and was off.

'Staying with you, is she?' Megan asked.

'For now. I don't know what her plans are. She makes her own moves as you see. How're you going with the quarries?'

'Okay. I think I've got them all and I'm plotting them on a map. I'm most of the way to tracking down who actually owns them.'

'And?'

'Tell you when I finish.'

She was wearing a bandanna around her head. I pointed to it.

'How's the wound?'

'Healing. My swim cap covers it and protects it neatly. Faint scar maybe. Doesn't worry me. Could be sexy.'

'Funny,' I said, 'I've never found that to be true.'

'You've probably got too many.'

I went into Hank's office and asked him what he was doing.

'Cleaning up a few things and working on getting some inside dope on Tarelton.'

'How?'

'I've located the guy who installed their computer network.'

'That'd be a shocking breach of confidentiality.'

'Wouldn't it? I like our client. She says she'll back us all the way.'

I nodded. 'Question is, how far will we get?'

'Think positive. What're you doing?'

'Working on a hunch.'

'Oh, yeah? Be secretive. Secretive is good.'

My notes had not looked wrong-headed in the morning. Rather the reverse. I phoned Josephine Dart.

'Mr Hardy. I've seen the reports about Henry. Do you have any other news?'

'I'm afraid not, but I'd like to see you. Today, if possible.'

She sighed. 'I anticipated that. Yes, you can come here, now if you wish.'

I thought I might've been met with reluctance, but not so. She sounded almost relieved, and I had a feeling that perhaps I was making some progress as I drove to Dover Heights again. She met me at the door as before but her manner was very different. Defensive? Apprehensive?

The flat had the same appealing lived-in look with a touch of neglect at the edges. Josephine Dart was dressed as before, simply and elegantly, but with strain showing in her face. I wasn't offered coffee. We stood in front of those windows full of blue sky and grey-green sea.

'You know, don't you?'

'I'm only guessing.'

'I gave you something to guess with, didn't I?'

'Secrets are hard to keep and they don't always do you any good. Just a few things you said had me wondering.'

'It's a relief, actually. So just a few words steered you in the right direction?'

'Not really,' I said. 'When I sat down to think about it, Henry McKinley came across as just too good to be true.'

'He was my lover.'

I nodded. 'Did your husband know?'

She smiled. 'Oh, so you're only halfway there.'

She turned away from the window and walked across to a drinks tray I hadn't seen on my last visit. She dropped ice cubes into two glasses and poured solid slugs of scotch. She held the drink out towards me in a hand that barely shook.

'Have a drink,' she said. 'Yes, Henry was my lover and Terry knew because they were lovers, too. And there were others.'

part two

12

It all came out in a rush. The Darts and McKinley had been involved in a ménage à trois with a difference, in that McKinley was the lover of both partners in the marriage. The arrangement had started almost ten years before, she said, and had continued happily right up until McKinley's disappearance.

'Are you shocked, Mr Hardy?'

'Nothing shocks me except reality television and house prices.'

She smiled. 'A man of the world.'

'You said there were others.'

'Yes, occasionally. Another man, or another woman. I wasn't going to have both hands tied behind *my* back, if you follow me.'

'And no friction, ever?'

'Scarcely ever, and then it was quickly overcome.'

'I don't mean between you three. I meant from the others.'

'Only once. A few years back. A man Henry met some-where. He joined us a few times but he became . . . possessive.'

'Of who?'

'Of me. Terry and Henry persuaded him that his behaviour was unacceptable. I believe he protested but he didn't persist.'

'Do you know his name?'

'Oh, no. No names. No real names.'

I looked around the flat. 'Easy enough to find out who you were.'

'You don't imagine we had . . . meetings here or at Henry's place when there were others involved?'

'Where then?'

'Why?'

'I need to know everything I can about Dr McKinley's movements.'

'Yes, I see. Well, at Myall on the lower north coast. A house there—leased in a false name. We were careful. What do you have in mind?'

'I have to take a look at any place McKinley spent time at. He might have left things . . .'

'I suppose it's possible. He went up there on his own from time to time. I'll give you the address. You already have the key.'

I'd wondered about that extra key. 'How long has the lease got to run?'

She shrugged. 'About a year. We . . . it was renewed recently. We never thought . . .'

'Are you planning to go there?'

She looked at me as if I'd uttered an obscenity. 'No, never again!'

She gave me the address and saw me to the door.

'So you're going to keep working. Do you need money?'

I told her that Margaret McKinley was in Sydney and

would finance the investigation. Her tiny hand flew to her mouth.

'You'll tell her about . . . us?'

'I'm not sure. If I have to.'

'We did nothing wrong,' she said defiantly. 'We hurt no one.'

'I hope that's true,' I said.

I sat in the car and thought about it. Wife-swapping seemed like an eighties thing, but this wasn't exactly that. More bizarre, or more under control? It was difficult to say. But the information opened up new lines of enquiry. What if Henry McKinley's extracurricular activities had opened him up to blackmail from some quarter—a colleague, a rival? What if Terry Dart had nursed a grudge, a jealousy, unknown to his wife—wanting exclusive possession of her or McKinley— and had eliminated his lover by accident or design?

And what of the man who hadn't played the game, whoever he was? Josephine Dart had a special, fragile allure. It was easy to imagine someone becoming obsessed with her, particularly in the context of a sexual free-for-all. Could he have killed McKinley and Dart and be biding his time?

I had the problem of whether or how to tell Margaret. There was a chance she wouldn't believe it—see it as a fantasy dreamed up by a grieving woman. I didn't think it was that. The Myall address gave the story solidity and had to be checked out. I had a memory flash of Lily sitting at her computer, working on a story and looking up at me as I brought her a drink.

'This thing opens up like a fucking fan,' she'd said one time.

I knew what she meant. I decided to wait until I knew what Margaret's moves were. She had to consult the lawyer; there was the release of her father's body to be negotiated and a funeral to arrange. She had enough on her plate. The Myall expedition could wait.

Margaret sailed into the arrangements with tremendous efficiency. Horace Greenacre had shown her the will naming him and Margaret as executors. McKinley, a firm atheist, had insisted on a secular send-off with a minimum of fuss and cremation. Margaret put one of those no flowers/ donations to the Fred Hollows Foundation notices in the paper.

Greenacre, several members of the cycling club and Ashley Guy from Tarelton attended the Rookwood chapel. A couple of suits I didn't know were there. Cops? Josephine Dart didn't show. A tallish, thin woman in a dark dress and jacket arrived late and didn't stay long. Margaret and the leader of the club spoke briefly and some of Henry's favourite music was played—Mozart, Vivaldi, Bach.

Not enough bodies for a wake or a proper party. Margaret thanked each person individually. They took off, leaving just Margaret and me.

'Well,' she said. 'That was a fizzer. I couldn't even cry.'

'Pretty cold,' I agreed, 'but it doesn't really matter. You've got strong memories, haven't you?'

We crunched across the gravel to my car. I was too hot in my suit, the only dark one I have. I peeled off the jacket; my shirt was sticking to my back. Margaret was cool in a blue dress. The only black thing about her was her handbag.

'Memories, yes,' she said, 'good ones but not that strong. He was away so much, always working. I'm not sure that I really knew him.'

We got into the car and she leaned across and gave me another of her low-octane kisses.

'Tell you what, Cliff, Dad's favourite tipple was single malt scotch on one block of ice. I vote we buy a bottle and have a few. I feel like getting pissed.'

I overruled that. We went back to Glebe and I shed the suit. We got a taxi to the Rocks and had the scotches in one of the new, trendy licensed cafes. We walked around for a while and then had a seafood meal with a lot of wine. Then Irish coffee. She insisted on paying.

'I'm coming into quite a lot of money,' she said, spearing a chunk of swordfish.

'Good.'

'Puts college for Lucinda beyond doubt.'

We discussed Lucinda; we discussed Megan; we discussed Lily and Margaret's ex-husband. We talked politics and books until it got quite late and the emotion, such as it was, of the day and the alcohol got to her and we caught a taxi to Glebe. She leaned against me and I put my arm around her on the way.

At home she asked for more coffee. She said goodnight and I heard the shower running long and hard, first cold then hot—different sounds. I showered in the downstairs bathroom and went up to bed, thinking I might manage a chapter of McGrath. It was a sleep-between-the-sheets night with a fan on and I'd just got settled when the door opened and Margaret came in.

She was wearing just the top of her silk pyjamas and the buttons weren't fastened.

'This is silly,' she said. 'I like you and you like me, don't you?'

'Very much.'

'Move over.'

She slid into bed and we made love slowly and carefully, each learning what the other liked and needed. When we finished we lay close together with only a film of sweat between us.

'Was that your first time since the heart attack?'

'Yes. I'm behind schedule. The hospital pamphlet said you could resume after six weeks.'

She laughed. 'I think most men start solo.'

'I thought about it but decided it was immature.'

We were drowsily quiet for a while; then she took my hand and said, 'You know I'm going back to the States, don't you? This is just . . .'

'It's what it is. I know. Nothing to say I can't visit though. Tony'll be fighting for the title soon. What d'you think about boxing?'

'I don't. What do you think about basketball?'

'I don't.'

'Right, I'll come and watch Tony if you'll come and watch the Lakers.'

We rolled apart and drifted off to sleep. I woke first and enjoyed the sight of her sleeping. She had her hand held up near her head, making her look oddly young and vulnerable. I eased out of the bed, showered and put on an old cotton dressing gown. She was still asleep and I put her kimono on the bed and went downstairs to make coffee and listen to the news, get the paper in, start the day.

She came down in her pyjama top and kimono. She kissed me. 'How's that Cold Chisel song go?'

I recited:

The coffee's hot
And the toast is brown.

'That's it. I loved that group. Is "Sweethearts" still there?'
I poured her coffee and put the bread in the toaster.
'I don't know. We'd better find out.'

She pointed to the paper. 'What's the news?'

I showed her the headline: GOVERNMENT IN DEEP TROUBLE!

'That's weeks away,' she said. 'Things change.'

The toaster popped and I put the slices on a plate and pushed them towards her with the margarine and the honey.

'The government's shot to bits in the polls,' I said. 'They figure they need time to turn it around.'

'Reckon they can?'

'No.'

'Good. Why're we talking about this and not about finding out who killed my dad? I know it's important, politics, but . . .'

I got orange juice from the fridge and detached my pills from their foils. I swilled a couple down and then dropped the aspirin tablet into a glass of water, watched it dissolve and drank it. The taste was sweetish and unpleasant. I followed it with a mouthful of coffee.

'It's not all that important,' I said. 'Be good to see the last of the present lot, but things'll change only at the margins.'

'Cliff, come on. You're stalling.'

'Right,' I said. 'Things to tell you.'

13

I told her what Josephine Dart had told me. She listened without interrupting, but she left her toast practically untouched. When I'd finished she drank her coffee which must have been tepid.

'And you believed her?' she said.

'I think so.'

'You think.'

I'd made copies of the three keys that had got me into McKinley's townhouse and the one to the shed padlock. I'd given the copies to the police who'd made a search after the discovery of McKinley's body. The fifth key had puzzled me, as I'd told Mrs Dart. I got the original set from my jacket and singled out the fifth key.

'She had keys to your father's house,' I said. 'This one is allegedly the key to the place at Myall. She says the house hasn't been used since her husband's death, not by her anyway. If what she says is true there should be signs of their . . . activities, and it's possible your father might have left something there that could make sense of what happened to him. Just possible.'

She nodded. 'You see, it's as I said before. I didn't really know him. If this is true I'm glad in a way. I never liked to think of him alone and sexless. Pedalling away the frustration. I suppose I was thinking of a nice female companion, someone I'd like, but you can't legislate for people's sex lives, can you?'

'No way known so far.'

'So when're we going up there to take a look?'

Before setting off for the coast, we went in to Newtown to tell Hank and Megan the latest.

'Jesus,' Hank said, 'that opens up a can of worms.'

'Ugly image,' Margaret said.

Hank said, 'Sorry, Ms McKinley, I . . .'

Margaret smiled. 'Margaret, remember?'

Megan watched this exchange with amusement. As far as I could tell, Margaret and I presented exactly as before, but some women can read signs not apparent to most. She was fighting to repress a knowing smile.

'Any quarries up there?' I asked, just to deflect her.

She went to her desk and shuffled paper. 'There is as it happens—Larson's quarry at a place called Howard's Bend, not that far away.'

She tapped keys and the printer spewed out a sheet.

'Bit of a mystery this,' Megan said. 'Mind you, most of them are. Ownership or leasehold has to be tracked through a minefield of interlocking companies. I'm struggling, I admit. But you might check this one out physically. Why not?'

I took the sheet and folded it. We left.

'She knows we're fucking,' Margaret said when we reached the street.

'Yes. She—'

A movement across the street took my attention and I caught a glimpse of Phil Fitzwilliam in a car pulled up at a set of lights. He looked my way and then said something to his driver as the car accelerated away, jumping the red light.

'What?' Margaret said.

'Nothing. Just saw someone I don't want to see.'

'I suppose you've got a few enemies?'

'A few.'

'But friends as well, right? Who's this Frank Parker you talk about?'

'He's my best friend, and he outweighs quite a few enemies.'

We took my car because Margaret said she wasn't confident about driving any great distance on the wrong side of the road. She was worried about the turns on and off the bridge.

'I can just see the headline,' she said. '"Expat driver causes pile-up on bridge".'

We'd originally planned to go up and back in the one day, but Megan's quarry would take up some time, so we stopped in Glebe and packed overnight bags. In the past I'd have taken a pistol, even on a benign trip like this, but I didn't have a licensed firearm anymore, or an unlicensed one. The last illegal gun I'd had I'd thrown into the harbour after I'd tried to kill a man—Lily's murderer—with it. The gun had jammed, for which I was eternally grateful. I packed a camera instead.

Myall was about 200 kilometres north-west of Sydney. I'd never been there but the directions I'd got from the web seemed easy enough. Drive about 70 kilometres north of Newcastle and then 10 kilometres off the Pacific Highway. The village, the region, were named for the Myall Lakes, where I seemed to remember there'd been important archaeological digs in the past. I'd forgotten the details. Something significant about stone axes and the length of time the Aborigines had been in the country—longer than anyone thought.

Margaret and I chatted about these sorts of things on the drive. I played an Edith Piaf CD and one of the best of Cold Chisel and we pledged to find out about 'Sweethearts'. The Falcon, recently tuned up, performed well and I enjoyed the first decent stint I'd had at the wheel since the heart episode. We had a rest stop just north of Newcastle—light beers and salad sandwiches. Time was when a country salad sandwich was white bread with a thick layer of butter, a slice of tomato, a slice of beetroot and some limp lettuce; mayonnaise if you were lucky. These were California style—wholemeal rolls with your choice of almost everything. There are things we should thank America for.

Margaret took over the driving. 'I haven't driven a stick shift in years,' she said.

'We call it a manual.'

'Whatever. Be a challenge not to stall it.'

She didn't. The secondary road was good and we followed it to a bridge across the Myall River, skirted the towns on either side and followed the road, not as good now, west beside the river for a couple of kilometres. The guide books described Myall as a 'village' and that's what it was, if not a hamlet. It consisted of about twenty houses that all seemed to be hiding from each other, a general store and a boat and fishing gear hire establishment beside the jetty. Not my idea of a holiday destination but I don't fish. The river had muddy banks and mangroves.

The house was up a gravel stretch bearing an amateurish sign reading 'Mosquito Track'.

'Great,' Margaret said, 'just what we need—a dose of Ross River fever. I can't see Dad up here, there's nowhere to cycle.'

He wasn't here to cycle, I thought, but said nothing as she pulled up in front of a weatherboard cottage mostly hidden by thickets of lantana.

We went up an overgrown path to the front porch. From there I could see a couple of boats downriver but no other sign of activity. If privacy was what you wanted, this was it. The key worked and we stepped into a short hallway leading to a living room. The house had the musty smell of being closed up for a long while, plus touches of damp, dust and dead flies. The living room was comfortable with armchairs, a coffee table, well-stocked bookshelves and a television and CD player.

There were two bedrooms off the living room. I took the one on the right, Margaret took the other. The room I entered held a queen-sized bed with a black satin cover. There were mirrors attached to the walls adjacent to the bed. A TV with DVD player stood at the end of the bed. A wardrobe held a variety of fetishist clothing—silk, satin, leather, latex items in sizes from very small to fairly large. The top drawers in the bedside chest contained an array of sex toys—dildos, masks, gags, restraints—and a variety of lubricants and condoms. The lower drawers held neat stacks of pornographic DVDs.

I switched on the bedside lamp and got what

I expected—a red glow. I left the room and found Margaret sitting on a chair staring into space.

'Fun and games,' she said. 'A cross between what I imagine a brothel and a dominatrix dungeon would be like. I wonder where they keep the coke and the herb? I could do with a joint.'

I nodded. 'Same in the other room. Nothing really cruel though, and signs of care being taken. No harm done with everyone willing.'

'You're right. It's just a bit hard to take in, when it's your parent.'

'Mine would've got along a lot better with a bit of the same,' I said. 'Well, Josephine Dart was telling the truth.'

Margaret smiled. 'I wonder how she's going to deal with all the accoutrements when the lease runs out.'

'She might renew.'

'You say she said she loved my dad. I'd like to meet her, I think.'

'She's impressive in a brittle kind of way.'

Margaret jumped up. 'Give me a kiss.'

We kissed close and hard.

'Have you ever been into stuff like this?' she asked.

'Skirted the edges once or twice. It didn't do a lot for me.'

'Mm, I had a brief dyke phase after my husband split but it didn't take.'

We broke apart and went out to the kitchen. It was mid-twentieth century style with lino, laminex and formica, and a hot water tank over the sink. But it had the right modern fittings—a microwave, dishwasher and gas stove. Margaret opened a few cupboards and found them well stocked with tinned and packet food and jars containing rice, sugar and flour. She pointed to the jars.

'Dad was a great one for that,' she said. 'We lived in this old house at first and had to watch out for rats.'

I opened a cupboard and found bottles of whisky, brandy and rum. The fridge held bottles of soda and tonic along with gin and vodka and vermouth. There was tomato and orange juice and a jar of olives.

'They did themselves proud,' I said.

Margaret sniffed at the opened carton of milk and made a face. She leaned against the sink, suddenly looking tired. 'Why're we here, Cliff? With all this sex and jollity, I kind of forget.'

'To see if your father left anything to suggest . . .'

'What killed him. Right. Where d'you you think we should look? Maybe under the beds—or in them? Come on, Cliff, they did nothing here but screw in various combinations.'

I pointed to the cup, glass and spoon on the draining rack. 'Mrs Dart said your father sometimes came here on his own,' I said. 'These're probably his.'

She shrugged. 'I want to get away from here. Let's go look at the bloody quarry.'

'Bear with me.' It seemed unlikely that McKinley would put anything of professional importance in the boudoirs or the kitchen. I took a quick look at the bathroom—neat, tidy, no hiding places. That left the living room. I worked through the bookshelves while Margaret sat, sceptically fiddling with a strand of hair. Nothing.

How do you store data? I thought, trying to put myself in the scientist's shoes. I wasn't sure. *How do you best hide something?* I knew the answer to that—where everyone can see it. There was a rack of DVDs under the player—movies, documentaries. I finger-picked my way through them and in the middle found an unlabelled disc.

'What's that?' Margaret said. 'Their home movies? I don't think I want to see it. Maybe I do.'

'I don't know.' I turned on the TV, put the disk into the DVD player and pressed PLAY.

14

McKinley appeared on screen and Margaret gave a gasp.

'He looks so old and sick,' she murmured.

He was in his study, swivelled around in his chair to face the camera. A sheaf of notes sat on his desk. He spoke in a strong, clear voice, at odds with his eroded, almost fragile appearance. 'I want to place on record something of my recent researches and some of the problems that have been thrown up. I was commissioned by Edward Tarelton to investigate the possibility of tapping into the vast aquifer that lies beneath the Sydney basin. This contains an incalculable volume of pure water, access to which could solve urban Sydney's water problem long into the future.

'The existence of this water has been known for a very long time and many geologists and other scientists have attempted to find a method of utilising it. Parts of the deposit have been tapped apparently successfully but problems of subsidence have arisen as a result. Buildings have cracked and require stabilisation. This will continue. However, my investigations reveal that the greater part of the aquifer is sealed off from the portions that have been tapped and remain intact and undisturbed. A heavy, apparently impenetrable layer of sandstone overlays the main body of the aquifer. Any attempt to blast through this layer, even in the event of its highly unlikely success given the density and thickness of the layer, would result in the release of the water under such pressure that no monitoring device could control it.

'I believe I have a found a site where the aquifer could be safely tapped, given a very considerable investment of capital, the carrying out of a meticulous environmental impact survey, and the employment of highly trained and principled technicians. I've also devised the correct technique for the operation to be done safely. Under the terms of my contract—a secret agreement entered into between Tarelton Explorations and myself to preserve confidentiality—I am obliged to provide this information to the company. I have not done so. In fact, after I became aware of certain things, I have provided misleading and erroneous information.'

I hit PAUSE.

'Jesus,' Margaret said, 'this is big. Have you ever heard of this aquifer thing?'

'All I know about it is what I'm learning now.'

I pressed PLAY again.

'The confidentiality I spoke of has been breached,' McKinley went on. 'And I believe there are now two other organisations who are aware of my researches and have received the preliminary, positive reports I tendered to Tarelton. This information has come to me through a source I trust—one of my research assistants at Tarelton—Susan O'Neil. According to Dr O'Neil, Tarelton has entered into agreements with Lachlan Enterprises and

Global Resources in violation of my agreement with Tarelton.

'My own subsequent enquiries suggest that all three companies have serious and suspect political connections and are more like rivals than cooperative partners. Perhaps Edward Tarelton has made a mistake in recruiting the others. I assume he needs the capital. But the upshot is that I no longer feel prepared to report in full on my research. I now believe that whatever organisation possesses this data will use it to circumvent legal requirements and will attempt to exploit the aquifer for purely selfish, commercial purposes.

'Serious environmental damage and harm to large sections of residential and business areas would result from irresponsible tapping and exploitation of what I call the greater aquifer.

'Again, this is clearly contrary to my arrangement with Tarelton, which was that all legal conditions governing the aquifer would be met, with the company deriving an appropriate reward, but no more. The state government has the rights to the deposit, but may make arrangements for its use. I fear that political and commercial considerations may override ethics at this point. I was excited by the research project, seduced by the funds and expertise available to me and I was naïve.'

I paused the disc again. 'This is heavy stuff,' I said. 'He's talking about three competitors, all looking to make dodgy millions from his work done in good faith. Sorry, Margaret, I'm really talking to myself. Trying to get a handle on this.'

Margaret said, 'Each one of them with reasons to steal what he discovered or . . . kill him. I need a drink.'

She went out to the kitchen and came back with two glasses—solid scotches with water. 'Go on,' she said.

McKinley's frozen image came to life again. 'I have reason to believe that these . . . competing forces, shall I call them, are aware of my hesitation and will continue, in their different ways, to bring pressure to bear. I have been virtually threatened by Tarelton and Lachlan and offered a ridiculous inducement by Global Resources, which I refused, not that there was any possibility of their actually paying it.

'I believe my life is in danger and I am trying to think of a secure way to document the site and the technique so that the legal and ethical standards can be met. I haven't yet come up with one and I'm making this record just to . . . I suppose protect myself. I'm confused and unwell. The strain of this problem has affected my health, which has always been excellent. I am short of breath and subject to episodes of fatigue quite unfamiliar to me.

'I've thought of approaching the police, but one of the threats I mentioned actually came from a police officer and I know that at least two of the involved companies have corrupt senior government ministers working in their interest. I'm considering going higher, but water is now such a political, moral and environmental touchstone that I don't know who to trust . . .'

Margaret covered her eyes with one hand and gestured for me to stop the recording.

'Poor, poor Dad,' she said. 'Why didn't he hop on a plane and . . .'

I shook my head. 'I suspect he was aware of being watched, and the last thing he would have wanted would be to draw you and Lucinda into the mess.'

She nodded and flapped her hand. 'Go on, please.'

'The data is not electronically recorded,' McKinley

continued. He gestured at the notes on his desk. 'And I propose to burn these documents. I want to find a way to communicate my findings personally to a trustworthy person or organisation but I'm not hopeful. This records my sincere desire to do the right thing. I hope my beloved daughter and grand-daughter will become aware of that and think well of me.'

The screen went blank. Margaret sobbed uncontrollably.

In the past, people paid a lot of attention to fireplaces. Now, we regard them as ornamental, and I hadn't even noticed that the living room had one. As Margaret regained self-control, I went over to the fireplace: the grate was full of ashes, clearly the remnants of many sheets of paper. Henry McKinley had done what he said he would do and his multimillion dollar information had been locked up inside his head. The question was—had anyone forced the information from him and, if so, who?

Margaret took a strong pull on her drink and watched me as I poked at the ashes in the vain hope that the destruction hadn't been complete.

'He was a brave man,' I said.

'He was a bloody fool. The corruption here can't be that bad. Why didn't he go to the media?'

'Look, as he says, he was bound by a legal agreement. If he went to the media they'd be wary about that and take some time over it, then stuff could leak out and he could be in all sorts of trouble. His credibility could be shot. He shouldn't have destroyed the notes, though. That put the entire burden on him and he didn't look well enough to handle it.'

Margaret finished her scotch and went out to the kitchen for the bottle. She freshened both drinks. 'Do you think we'll ever find out what happened?'

'We can try. This Dr O'Neil is someone we have to talk to, and I've got an idea who the policeman he mentioned might be.'

She didn't pursue that and for a minute I thought she might have resigned herself to no result and be looking for a way to tell me so. But I was wrong.

'I still think that drawing is a quarry,' she said, 'and now that we've heard what Dad said it makes more sense, doesn't it? A quarry's a big, deep hole, right? That would make a good start at getting down to the water, wouldn't it?'

'Could be.'

'I want to see the quarry around here. I want to see all the fucking quarries. If we find one that fits the drawing, that's a start on what he was on about. Grab the disc and let's go, Cliff. I want to get out of this place.'

'Is there anything of your dad's here—books or CDs—that you might want to keep, d'you think?'

She shook her head and held up the scotch bottle. 'Just this.'

Margaret used the toilet. I went outside and scouted around the house. The grass was getting out of control, leaves were building up here and there and some rubbish—plastic bottles and fast food containers—had been trapped in the bushes. Bending to examine a yellowed copy of the local newspaper, I found a pair of spectacles in the grass. Expensive, and exactly like those worn by Henry McKinley. I wrapped them in a tissue and shoved them into my jacket pocket.

* * *

Being thorough, Megan had ranged far and wide in her researches. Larson's quarry was about sixty kilometres south-west of Myall and the drive took us along the river for a stretch, crossing it and heading into the drier country away from the coast. The road got rougher as we entered the stony uplands around Barkley's Ridge. The air got cooler and the Falcon coughed a bit on the climb. We passed through the town of Barkley that had once had a rail link to the coast, long since closed. We threaded through some hills on a road that had in the past been wide and well maintained but had degenerated to little more than a track.

'I hope your tyres are good,' Margaret said. It was almost the first time she'd spoken since leaving Myall.

'Brand new,' I said.

The land flattened out into sparse grazing country and we crossed a couple of streams on bridges originally built to handle much greater water volumes and now looking too large for the sluggish, weed-choked creeks. We passed through a township only a little bigger than Myall named Howard's Bend. Further on the road sloped down suddenly and stopped beside a body of water about the size of ten Olympic swimming pools. The water shimmered a deep cobalt blue under the clear sky.

'Larson's quarry,' I said.

'It's nothing like Dad's drawing,' she said, 'but it's pretty, isn't it?'

She was right—the rectangular, water-filled hole, with trees growing high around three of its sides, didn't resemble Henry McKinley's drawing in the least. Although his creation was more or less an abstract, surely he would've suggested the trees and the water. But it *was* pretty. Megan's notes said that the quarry had provided 'building material'

for inland and coastal towns. Now it provided welcome
visual relief from a basically sterile landscape.

We got out of the car and walked down to the edge.
The quarry had steep slopes on three sides, but here the
gravel slope was gradual to water that looked no more than
waist-deep. There were reeds sprouting at the edge and
pelicans and ducks moved sedately on the surface. Looking
at the quarry, I was suddenly aware of how rare it is these
days to see a body of water unfenced, apart from the ocean
and the rivers. Margaret must have had a parallel thought.

'I wonder if it'd be OK to swim?'

'Can't see why not. If it's on private property there's no
sign against trespassing and the water's clean. Looks to have
a firm bottom.'

Margaret took her clothes off, folded them neatly, and
waded out into the water. She dived, surfaced and struck
out in a strong, practised crawl for the deeper water. I did
the same and joined her, treading water while the birds
moved cautiously away.

'Bloody freezing,' I said.

'But beautifully clean, just what I needed. Let's have a
look at your scar. Didn't get a chance the other night.'

She examined the line running down the centre of my
chest, kissed it and then put her hands on my shoulders and
ducked me. When I surfaced she was halfway back to
the edge. We left the water, both shivering, and I scooted to the
car to get my gym towel. We shared it, sweat-smell and all.

She pointed to the scar as I pulled on my shirt.

'Dr Pierce did a great job. Pity he's so pompous.'

'Pompous is OK with me in his case.'

'Let's find a motel,' Margaret said. 'I want to fuck you.'

* * *

We booked into a motel in Barkley and began making love as soon as the door closed behind us. We didn't pretend not to be stimulated by the erotica in the Myall cottage. The refreshing swim gave us energy to go with heightened feelings. We tried different positions and prolonged the pleasure.

'I hope you do visit,' Margaret said when we finished for the first time.

'I will,' I said.

I hadn't told her about finding the glasses. Henry McKinley had been taken from the Myall cottage. It made sense. He couldn't risk leaving the DVD at his house where either Tarelton or its competitors would surely search, and he'd been right about that. He'd assumed that no one but his lovers knew about the Myall cottage and that if they found the disc they'd do the right thing with it. He'd been mistaken. His predators knew about the Myall retreat. These days, big money employers know everything.

After we'd made love again, Margaret fell asleep and I lay thinking. McKinley had been taken and killed but he'd left a crucial piece of evidence behind. In a way, he'd had the last laugh. I'd try to put it that way to Margaret.

15

Next day, in Sydney, Margaret went shopping for a gift for her daughter and I reported on our progress to Hank and Megan. I didn't go into details about the set-up in the cottage, but I told them about the ashes, the glasses and that I thought Myall was where McKinley had been abducted. Then I played the DVD for them.

'This is big,' Hank said.

'Too big.' Megan had been scribbling notes. 'This has to be handled by the police or ICAC or someone.'

'I don't know,' I said. 'If it becomes known what McKinley was doing and the suspicions he had, the three players will shut up shop, run the shredders, call off the dogs. The only way to find out which of them was responsible for McKinley's death is to keep alive their hopes of getting their hands on his research.'

'That's assuming he didn't tell them when they had him,' Megan said.

'Right. But we may have an insider in this Dr O'Neil. If she's still working for Tarelton, she'll know whether they've hit pay-dirt or not.'

'Have to find a way to talk to her privately,' Hank said.

'Maybe not.'

Megan looked at me. 'You'd set her up?'

'It's worth thinking about, but probably not. At least not straight off.'

Megan closed her notebook. 'I see now why some people call you a bit of a bastard.'

'Only some people; only a bit of one.'

When I got to the house I found Margaret agitated and packing.

'I have to go, Cliff,' she said. 'It's not working out with Lucinda and her dad. They've had a row and she's very upset. I'm on a flight in a couple of hours.'

'I'm sorry. I'll drive you. Is she with someone?'

'Yes, yes, she's OK. Thanks, Cliff. You're right, that's the important thing, she's OK.'

I drove her to the airport and we had time for a quick drink before her flight, inevitably delayed, was called. She'd calmed down by this time and was able to think of other things beside her kid.

'I want you and Hank and Megan to keep on with this until you find out what happened.' She reached for my hand. 'But don't do anything dangerous. I want to see you again, Cliff.'

The flight was called. I walked her to the gate and we kissed and hugged hard and seriously. Then she disappeared into Customs. I didn't try to watch the take-off. With planes coming in and going out at the rate they do it's impossible to tell one from another. And what's the point? Gone is gone. I went back to the bar for another overpriced whisky and as I drank it I could smell a faint trace of her perfume on my jacket. It made me feel lonely, but it made me feel determined to find out who'd beaten or frightened Dr Henry McKinley to death.

After the drink I walked around the airport for half an hour for the exercise and to metabolise the alcohol. It didn't help the loneliness, but it didn't hurt the determination.

'How do you feel about cycling, Cliff?' Megan asked when I turned up at the office the next day. I'd told her about Margaret. I'd been to the gym and felt fine, but not that fine.

'Here and now? In Sydney? Roughly how I feel about skydiving. Why?'

Hank and Megan had done their thing on the internet. No one's safe. They'd tracked Susan Talbot O'Neil from her stellar HSC result, when she was one of three who'd got the highest score in the state, through to her University Medal for Science at Sydney to her Cambridge PhD in geology.

'Guess who examined her thesis?' Megan said.

'Henry McKinley.'

'Right. He seems to have lured her away from a research post at the ANU to the corporate sector, specifically Tarelton Explorations.'

'More money.'

'Lots more, but also more her kind of thing.'

'Water.'

'And how it got to where it is and how to get it out. But wait, there's more.'

Megan was grinning and Hank gave her a high-five sign on the way back to his office.

'Dr O'Neil lives in Darling Point and her main recreation, at which she's won prizes by the way, is cycling. She's a member of the Four Bays Cycling Club.'

'Like McKinley.'

'Right. You're a little late today, but they do an early morning ride every day. We can pick them up at the clubhouse tomorrow around seven-thirty.'

'We?'

'With Margaret gone don't you think you need a woman's touch, as it were?'

She got on with researching the two other companies McKinley had mentioned while I thought about Phil Fitzwilliam. I hadn't told anyone about him, thinking that he was my problem. It seemed likely that he had some connection with the business at hand. His threat to Hank's licence wasn't just out of personal enmity and spite. I tried to see his approach as an opportunity, and to think of a way to turn it to our advantage. So far, nothing had occurred to me.

My mobile rang. Horace Greenacre.

'Mr Hardy,' he said, 'Ms McKinley paid me a flying visit before she left and she insisted on signing a power of attorney in your favour. I tried to dissuade her but—'

'Hold on,' I said. 'I know what a power of attorney is and I'm as surprised as you seem to be, but why did you try to talk her out of it?'

'No offence, Mr Hardy, but there's a good deal of money involved. Henry McKinley's townhouse is a valuable property. He had substantial investments and a high level life insurance policy, plus superannuation benefits.'

I gripped the phone, wanting to throw the thing at the wall, and swore under my breath. Since the publicity surrounding the loss of my licence, I'd faced this sort of suspicion before. It had surfaced most strongly when I inherited half of Lily's considerable estate, and here it was again in similar circumstances. I fought to keep my voice somewhere near civil.

'Listen, Horace, my only interest in Margaret McKinley's assets is in making use of them to finance the investigation into her father's murder.'

'I didn't mean—'

'You meant a disgraced private enquiry agent is a crook by definition. Well here's some instructions for you in respect of your late client and his heir. You get in touch with me when there's something I have to do in Margaret's interest, and I get in touch with you when I need something. I'm making notes on this conversation and solicitors have been known to lose their tickets, just like PEAs. Are we clear? Good.'

I cut the call and looked up to see Megan staring at me. 'Aren't you supposed to avoid stress?'

'Aren't you supposed to be tapping keys? . . . Shit, sorry, love. That prick got under my guard.'

'Keep your right up, then,' she said.

The phone rang again and I picked it up, steeling myself to be polite. It was Greenacre.

'Mr Hardy, I'm sorry we got off on the wrong foot then. My apologies.'

'Accepted. How can I help you?'

'Well, it's rather curious. Ms McKinley was in a considerable hurry as she left and she almost knocked over another client of mine who was just arriving. She was polite, of course. He commented on her haste, her accent and good manners and asked who she was. I told him and he suddenly showed great interest. He said he knew her father and was very anxious to meet her. I told him she was leaving the country almost immediately and he was very put out. I asked if it was a business meeting he had in mind and he said it was. I said I might be able to help. That's why I'm calling you now—to see if you're willing to meet him.'

'I don't know,' I said. 'Who is he?'

'His name's William Holland; he's the CEO of a company called Global Resources.'

I drew in a breath that must have sounded odd to Greenacre because his voice was suddenly full of concern.

'Mr Hardy, are you all right?'

'I'm fine, thank you. Please give Mr Holland my mobile number and ask him to call me in, say, an hour.'

Greenacre said he would and I put the phone down to find Hank and Megan looking at me. I realised that I had a grin on my face of a kind they probably hadn't seen for a while. I glanced at my watch.

'What?' Hank said.

I explained what had happened and the implications and possibilities were obvious. If Global Resources was responsible for McKinley's death a meeting with Holland might make that clear. Or perhaps Holland knew who was responsible and had useful information.

'Why didn't you get him to call you straight away?' Megan said.

I looked at my watch. 'It's one thirty. Let's say he calls Holland straight off—said he will. I said an hour. Let's see how keen the CEO of Global Resources really is. I'm slipping out for a drink. What d'you think?'

'Cute,' Hank said.

Megan said, 'Try not to sound as smug as you look.'

16

At two thirty-three the phone rang.

'On the dot,' I said to Megan.

I answered. 'Hardy.'

'Mr Hardy, this is William Holland, I'm—'

'I know who you are, Mr Holland. What can I do for you?'

'I'd like for us to meet.'

'Why?'

'To discuss matters arising from the work the late Henry McKinley was engaged on.'

'What work would that be?'

'I think that's commercially confidential.'

'You mean you don't know.'

'I mean I only know a certain amount.'

'Here's something else you might not know. Margaret McKinley, Dr McKinley's daughter and heir, has enlisted the services of Bachelor Private Enquiry Incorporated to investigate her father's death. I'm an associate of Bachelor's.'

There was a pause before Holland said, 'No, I didn't know that.'

So Greenacre was only giving out selective information.

That was good. I'd talked the thing over with Hank and Megan in what was left of the hour after my brief visit to the pub. We'd agreed it was unlikely that the actual kidnappers and probable torturers of Henry McKinley would make the approach Holland had: unlikely, but not impossible. Also, McKinley, on the DVD, said Global Resources had tried a soft approach—a bribe. Didn't acquit them of responsibility, but it suggested they might be the ones to deal with. We had that one card to play—the bribe allegation. The trick would be to use it to find out more. Holland might know more about the focus of McKinley's work than we did.

It was a juggling act and a chess game. We needed to talk to Dr O'Neil before we talked to Holland.

'I'll call Ms McKinley in the States,' I said to Holland, 'and get back to you if you give me your number. I gather it's urgent?'

'Fairly urgent. I'll expect your call when?'

'Within forty-eight hours.'

He gave me the number and cut the call.

We grouped in Hank's office.

'What does he sound like?' Megan asked.

'Smooth. What have you found out about the company?'

'It's biggish. International. Mining interests mostly, particularly in South Africa. Your Mr Holland is the CEO of the Australian division rather than the whole show.'

'That's interesting,' Hank said. 'Always good to deal with someone who's answerable to someone else. Can give you an edge.'

'We're going to need it, unless we can learn something useful from Dr O'Neil. Megan and I can try to contact her tomorrow morning, but I think all three of us should go to the meeting with Holland. My guess is he'll have others along.'

'That's better,' Megan said. 'I want to go.'

'It's going to be a chess game,' I said.

Hank groaned. 'I'm lousy at chess.'

'Me, too,' I said.

'I'm pretty good,' Megan said.

I gave her one of my winning grins. 'Thought you might be. Your mother was.'

The Four Bays Cycling Club clubhouse turned out to be a garage, one of a set cut into a cliff on a street a block back from New South Head Road in Rose Bay. A roller door had the club name, only partly disfigured by graffiti, stencilled on it. Megan and I gathered there at seven twenty on a brisk morning with a sharp wind coming off the water.

'They ride for an hour,' Megan said, 'rain, hail or shine, and they cover a bloody lot of clicks.'

'Admirable. I wouldn't fancy the hills.'

'They thrive on them. Think of the Tour de France.'

'That's for money. More understandable. Here they come.'

A group of riders swept around a bend and headed towards us, pedalling fast on the flat stretch. At about a hundred metres out, they slowed and coasted the rest of the way. We could hear their voices carrying clearly on the morning air above the sounds of traffic and the stiff breeze. There were ten people in the group, including two women.

'She's the thin one with the red helmet,' Megan said.

'I recognise her. She put in a brief appearance at the funeral.'

The riders bunched up, shook hands, chatted and inspected their bikes. We walked over to where the woman Megan had singled out was making an adjustment to the strap on one of her pedals.

'Excuse me,' Megan said, 'Dr O'Neil?'

The woman pulled off her helmet and shook out her long, dark hair. She was good looking—thin-faced with large dark eyes. In her lycra outfit, she displayed a body without a gram of extra fat.

'Yes, I'm Susan O'Neil. Who—?'

Megan spoke quickly but quietly. 'Sorry to grab hold of you like this, but it's important that we talk with you. We've been hired by Margaret McKinley, Dr Henry McKinley's daughter, to investigate his death.'

She was still half occupied by the strap, still probably considering how she'd done on the ride, but now she stopped what she was doing and studied us closely. The other riders were filing into the garage and I could see the racks waiting for their bikes. They must have showers and changing rooms inside. Nice set-up.

'How do I know that's true?'

Greenacre had faxed a copy of the power of attorney document Margaret had signed. I produced it and my long-cancelled PEA licence. Megan had a Bachelor Enquiries card with her name on it.

I said, 'We know something of Dr McKinley's concern about the integrity or otherwise of Tarelton Explorations and other interested parties. We thought it safer to approach you away from your place of work.'

'Thank God for that.' Her dark, evaluating eyes shifted between us. 'You're father and daughter.'

'We are,' Megan said.

'I don't know why, but that helps me to believe you. Please wait until I rack the bike and get changed and then I'll be willing to talk to you.'

'Thank you,' Megan said.

'I should say I'll expect you to talk to me before I talk to you.'

She wheeled the bike away and was the last rider into the garage. The roller door came down.

'Game of chess,' Megan said.

Dr O'Neil came down a set of steps above the garage. She was wearing a dark blue pants suit like the one she'd worn at Rookwood, heels, grey blouse, carrying a smart leather drawstring bag. She used the remote to unlock a silver-grey Subaru parked in the street, and gestured for us to follow. The car had a device for securing a bicycle on the roof.

'Probably goes on hundred kilometre rides up and down mountains somewhere out bush,' I said as Megan started the engine. We were in her old VW 1500, a car she refused to part with—like me with my Falcon.

'I thought you liked athletic women.'

'I did, now I feel a bit outclassed.'

We followed the Subaru to Double Bay where it swung into a parking spot outside a coffee shop. Megan had to drive further to find a space. We walked back and Dr O'Neil was waiting for us at an outside table. She was nervous, fiddling with the packets of sugar, as we sat down.

'I'm betting you'd have a long black,' I said.

She smiled. 'You lose—super-strength cap and I sugar it. Those rides burn up the calories.'

'Would you go in and order, Cliff?' Megan said. 'We're on expenses, Dr O'Neil. Mine's a flat white.'

I did as directed. Bringing Megan was the right move. When I got back the two women were on first name terms and the earlier tension had dissipated.

'I've told Susan about Dr McKinley's DVD and his suspicions,' Megan said. 'And that you saw her at Dr McKinley's funeral.'

She smiled. 'Come to think of it, I saw you, too.'

'We've got a meeting lined up with a representative of Global Resources,' I said. 'Not sure what he's going to say, but . . .'

The coffee came and Susan O'Neil did as she said she would—shovelled sugar into her mug. 'I know what he'll say. He'll offer the world for information about the aquifer and how to get to it.'

I sipped at my long black; it was very good, and so it should have been at the price. 'What about the others—Lachlan and Tarelton?'

Susan shrugged. 'Don't know anything about Lachlan. All I know is that the bigwigs at Tarelton are going spare. Apparently the company borrowed a hell of a lot of money on the expectation that Henry would deliver and now they're caught in a debt trap. They're cutting staff. I'm going to save them the bother by handing in my notice when I can be sure I'll get what's due to me.'

'It'd be useful if we had more cards to put on the table when we meet the man from Global,' Megan said. 'Our only interest is finding out who killed Dr McKinley, but I'm sure his daughter would hold to his idea of not exploiting his work. Is there anything else you can tell us?'

'I don't think so.'

I decided to be blunt. 'Do you know the site and the technique?'

'No, I don't, thank God.'

She'd almost finished her coffee and was preparing to leave.

'Could it be a quarry?' Megan said.

Susan burst into laughter. 'A quarry? Don't be ridiculous. Did Henry leave a clue about a quarry?'

'Maybe,' I said.

She gathered up her bag. 'Would have been a red herring then. Didn't Henry say anything about his research procedure on the DVD?'

'Nothing,' Megan said.

Susan sat down again and went back to fiddling with the sugar. 'I wonder why not.'

'We should have told you,' Megan said. 'Cliff and Margaret found ashes in the fireplace in the cottage. He said he'd burnt all his notes. We weren't holding back, we just . . .'

Susan nodded. 'It's OK. He wiped his computer clean of the serious data and mine too before he went missing. I've had to cover up, pretend to be analysing his results. It's been a strain.'

'There *is* something else you can tell us, isn't there?' I said.

She nodded. 'I just don't know why . . .'

Megan's tone was sympathetic. 'We should have shown you the DVD. We still can. He mentions you in the best possible terms. We think his reticence was out of a wish to protect his daughter, and you, Susan.'

Susan was almost tearful. 'He was a lovely man. Great fun. I knew he liked me, but there was never the slightest word or gesture out of line.'

He had that area covered, I thought.

'We haven't heard a word to his discredit,' Megan said.

Susan stopped fiddling with the sugar. 'OK, here it is. Henry's real research was done from the air. That's why I laughed at the quarry suggestion. He didn't go burrowing around on the ground. He chartered a plane and he took photographs and he had a system for analysing them. I helped him, but I only dealt with his figures and his co-ordinates, comparing them with the geological record.'

I drained my cold coffee and sat back in my chair. 'Tarelton would have known about that.'

Susan shook her head. 'No. He worked on the ground first and presented some findings that got the execs excited. That's when he . . .'

'What?' I said.

'He chartered the flights himself. He didn't tell them shit.'

'But he told you,' Megan said.

'I found out. He put the photos into the system but I knew they weren't from official sources and they were brand new.'

'Don't tell me,' I said, 'the photos were all on the computers and they were wiped.'

'That's right.'

'And you were never able to pinpoint . . .?'

'No way. I'm sorry.'

'It's all right,' Megan said. 'That's all very useful. Are you sure you can carry on at Tarelton after all this?'

'Just.'

We started to move and I thought of one last question. 'Where did he catch the flights from?'

'You really are a detective,' Susan said. 'Bankstown airport.'

17

'Useful,' I said as Megan drove us back to Newtown.
'Mmm.'

'What's the matter?'

'I was just thinking what a shitty world it is.'

'Only parts of it.'

'Here's the possibility of a solution to the city's water crisis and the only people with any integrity, the only ones not trying to make money out of it, get screwed.'

'Yeah, but at least the greedy ones haven't made the money yet and maybe they never will.'

'You don't think Dr McKinley's site and other information'll ever be known?'

'He did a good job of wiping it off the record.'

Megan was quiet for a while, coping with the heavy traffic along Broadway. At a long traffic light stop she said, 'I was thinking there's a job for Hank here. Did you know he has a pilot's licence?'

'I didn't.'

'He knows the drill. He could go to Bankstown airport and perhaps locate the pilot McKinley hired and then find out the area he was interested in. Who knows? The pilot might even have copies of the photographs. It'd depend on what equipment was used.'

'You're keen to discover McKinley's secret are you, love? That's not our brief.'

'I care about the city. So should you and everybody else. No one's ever going to do anything about saving all the water that just runs into the sea, and the desalination plant's a crock of shit.'

'Wouldn't hurt for Hank to have a go,' I said.

Margaret emailed that she'd arrived safely, had her daughter with her, and had more or less sorted out the problems with her ex. She told me about the power of attorney and hoped I didn't find it too great a responsibility. I replied that I appreciated her trust in me and that we were making progress, but were still well short of a resolution.

She replied, confessing that she'd taken a photo of me with her cell phone without me knowing and had shown it to her daughter. Lucinda said I looked like an older, rougher version of Russell Crowe. I could live with that. Bit taller, though.

I phoned Global Resources and was put through to William Holland very speedily.

'Mr Hardy—very good to hear from you. How do things stand?'

'It's time for a meeting. Could you propose a venue?'

'Well, we have a well-equipped boardroom and—'

'I bet you do. We don't. We have a few cubbyholes. I like the idea of Horace Greenacre's place. He seemed to have a bit of space. Perhaps you could arrange that.'

'I'm sure I could. When do you suggest?'

'This evening.'

'That's very short notice.'

'You said it was urgent.'

'You're right, I did. Okay. I'll phone Horace. Shall we say seven o'clock?'

'Seven thirty,' I said, just to be annoying.

'Very well.'

'That's 19.30 hours.'

'You are a very irritating man, for someone who has been stripped of his private detective's licence.'

He hung up.

'The lawyer's place,' I said to Megan, 'at seven thirty. We get there about forty minutes late.'

'Why?'

'So we can watch the news—see how the water crisis is going.'

I spent the afternoon swimming slow laps in the Victoria Park pool and at the Marrickville gym where Tony Truscott was training. He looked sharp, and he told me the contracts for his title fight were being drawn up.

'I hope you'll be there, Cliff.'

'I will. Did I see you stumble just a fraction when you weren't quite sure where the ropes were?'

He grinned. 'You bastard. Yeah, have to get that right. Know the ring like your living room. He will. Did you?'

I laughed. 'Mate, in my last fight I saw the ropes looking up from the canvas. An old-time fighter told me he could smell where they were. Didn't have to look.'

'They moved slower back then.'

'You're right. Have you got a firm date?'

'These Yanks try to screw with your head. It's maybe this and maybe that. I don't take any notice. I'm fighting for Lily. That's all the focus I need.'

I nodded and threw a left lead at him that he picked off as if I was in slow motion.

Hank and I arrived at Double Bay separately, within a few minutes of each other. He was alone.

'Where's Megan?' I said.

He shrugged. 'She got a call just as we were leaving. Don't know what about. She said she'd take a cab and probably be a bit late.'

'That's OK,' I said. 'I'll tell them someone else is coming—keep them on their toes.'

We went up the stairs to Greenacre's suite. He wasn't there, but his secretary was.

'The other gentlemen are in the conference room,' she said. 'This way, please.'

We entered a room with a long table and high-backed chairs. There were paintings on the walls and a wet bar and coffee-making gear discreetly tucked behind some greenery. Soft, concealed lighting. Two men stood by a tall window looking out at the evening sky. Both wore dark suits. One had silver hair and the other, who was vaguely familiar, had no hair at all. Silver-hair turned around as we came in and moved towards us, his hand extended.

'I'm William Holland and this is my associate, Clive Dimarco.'

Hank shook the hand. 'Hank Bachelor, this is Cliff Hardy.'

I exchanged nods with both men. 'We have an associate of ours coming. She'll be along soon.'

Holland didn't like it but what could he do? 'Excellent,' he said. 'Let's get started here. Do either of you want anything to drink?'

Hank shook his head.

'Scotch,' I said. 'Ice only.'

Holland inclined his head. 'Clive, if you'll be so good, mineral water for me.'

'Sure.' Dimarco's New York accent was strong, unlike Hank's, which had been eroded by his time in Australia. He prepared the drinks, making a scotch for himself as least as solid as mine.

We were all on our feet and uncertain how to arrange ourselves. Eventually, Holland took a chair near the top of the table but not at its head, and we all sat.

Dimarco drank, took a miniature tape recorder from his pocket and put it on the table. 'I reckon we ought to have a record of this meeting.'

Hank had a similar device in the pocket of his denim jacket and he produced it with a flourish. 'I agree,' he said.

'I'll start the ball rolling,' Holland said after sipping his drink. 'We entered into an agreement with Tarelton Explorations to share the fruits of Dr Henry McKinley's research into . . .'

'Tapping the Sydney basin aquifer,' Hank said.

'Exactly. Unhappily, relations between us and Tarelton deteriorated over time and we feared that our interest, and I might say our investment—'

'You invested money in Tarelton itself or directly into McKinley's research?' The whisky was smooth, the sort of stuff I'd buy myself if I ever got used to being affluent.

'The former, with a clear understanding that Dr McKinley's work would be fully supported.'

'I think maybe Tarelton was playing you for a sucker,' Hank said. 'Our information is that they were borrowing money from other sources. Could be from this Lachlan Enterprises outfit.'

Holland and Dimarco exchanged concerned looks. 'We certainly weren't aware of that,' Holland said.

I said, 'OK, so we've each given the other some information. Our brief is to discover who killed McKinley—nothing more, nothing less. Any information on that?'

'Of course not,' Dimarco said. 'We at Global were completely shocked by his death.'

I was wondering why Megan hadn't showed up, but I had a flash and snapped my fingers. 'Now I've placed you. You were at the funeral.'

'Right. Paying our respects.'

'Only trouble with that is,' Hank said, 'we have a statement on DVD from Dr McKinley that he had no knowledge of any . . . subsidiary arrangements made by Tarelton.'

I drank the rest of the scotch. 'Yeah, and when he found out about them, he became worried. Didn't want to reveal what he'd discovered because he suspected that these commercial arrangements were designed to exploit the aquifer to the detriment, shall we say, of the public interest.'

Dimarco shook his head, pale, lumpy and glowing under the soft light. 'We knew nothing at all . . .'

'You're lying,' Hank said. 'We know from Dr McKinley's statement that Global offered him a substantial bribe for the information.'

Holland couldn't contain himself. 'This statement, this DVD—does he . . .?'

'Do you deny you offered him money?' I said.

Again, Dimarco and Holland exchanged looks. 'These are intricate commercial arrangements,' Dimarco said.

'We're negotiating, here,' Holland said, leaning forward. 'It's a rough and tumble world. If your . . . client is prepared to consider an offer . . .'

He'd missed the point, and I was ready to give him the sort of reply he wouldn't want to hear when the window behind him and Dimarco exploded. Glass flew around as a volley of shots poured in, hitting some electrical fitting and plunging the room into darkness.

Instinctively, Hank and I dived for the floor, but I could feel blood running down my face from where the flying glass had nicked it. Dimarco had dived sideways, knocking Holland from his chair.

'Hank,' I said, 'you OK?'

'Yeah. Untouched.'

'Dimarco?'

'I'm all right, but I think William's been hit.'

A light fitting was sputtering, sending out sparks. The heat triggered the smoke alarm and the sprinkler system. The room became a wet, howling mess as sirens sounded outside, drawing closer. A choking smoke filled the room and we started coughing and wiping at our eyes. Hank and I lifted Holland bodily and, with Dimarco kicking chairs out of the way and us crunching glass under our feet, we scrambled out of the room, down the corridor and reached the stairs.

The woman who'd let us in was standing on the stairs screaming and Dimarco yelled at her to shut up and get out of the way. She stumbled to the bottom, still screaming. Hank was supporting Holland's upper body and his clothes were getting soaked with blood. We got Holland out onto the footpath and my knees were about ready to give way when two paramedics took over.

part three

18

The next few hours were a shit storm of cops, firemen, paramedics and TV crews. William Holland had been hit, not by a bullet, but by a shard of glass that had taken a chunk from the side of his head, causing massive bleeding. Working under a rigged-up emergency light, the paramedics had stemmed the flow, loaded him onto a stretcher and rushed him to hospital.

Dimarco, Hank and I were soaked by the sprinklers, and Dimarco had a lot of blood on his Armani suit. A second batch of paramedics escorted us across the street, away from the blaze of flashing lights. Police were holding back reporters as the fire crew withdrew after making sure that the place wasn't going to burn.

A paramedic crouched by the bench where Dimarco, Hank and I were sitting and looked us over closely. He stood up, puzzled.

'You guys don't seem to be in shock,' he said.

Dimarco took a packet of cigarettes from his pocket and offered them around. The paramedic took one; Hank and I refused. 'I guess we've been under fire before,' Dimarco said.

'Is that right?'

A plain clothes detective had come up quietly. I was busy blotting my minor facial cuts with a wad of tissues, but I looked up when I heard the voice. It was Phil Fitzwilliam.

'You gentlemen, and I don't include you, Hardy, have some explaining to do.'

Dimarco whipped his mobile phone from his pocket. 'Not without my lawyer present.'

Hank produced his mobile, but didn't say anything.

'How about you, Hardy?' Fitzwilliam said. 'Are you going to call in that cunt Garner, like you always do?'

I stood up and shook some of the fragments of glass from my clothes. 'Gee, Phil, I thought you meant I didn't have to do any explaining, that I was free to go.'

Two more detectives—the one I'd seen with Fitzwilliam before, and another, looking as if he might be of equal or senior rank—had joined Fitzwilliam, who bit back whatever response he'd been going to make to my remark. 'Two of these men are known to me, Inspector—private enquiry agents; one disbarred, both of ill repute. I don't know the other man.'

Dimarco, quite recovered and poised, produced his card. 'Clive Dimarco, vice-president of Global Resources.'

The man Fitz had deferred to was about his age but in much better physical condition. His suit was good without being too good, and he held himself like a man used to being listened to, not needing to bully—unlike Fitz. He ignored Dimarco's card.

'I'm Detective Inspector Sean Wells. You're going to have to accompany us to Surry Hills to answer—'

He stopped as I brushed him aside. Megan had got through the police barrier somehow and was hurrying towards us. Out of the corner of my eye, I saw Horace

Greenacre arguing fiercely with a cop, pointing at Megan. I could feel Hank thrusting forward but I sensed Fitzwilliam interposing his bulk.

Megan looked me with a depth of concern she'd never shown before, not even back in San Diego.

'Cliff, you're bleeding! Hank, are you OK? What happened? I'm sorry, I . . .'

Hank put his arms around her.

Looking down I saw that my shirt was splattered with blood. I said, 'It's OK, just a few scratches. Looks worse than it is. Someone broke up our meeting. It's a good thing you weren't there, but what kept you?'

'My sister, half-sister, rang. She wanted to get back in touch. I couldn't stop her yakking, and then I couldn't get a cab.'

Fitzwilliam was glowering, and Wells was looking aggressively in the direction of the TV crews.

'We have to go to Surry Hills,' I said. 'Shots were fired.'

'My God!'

Hank handed her his car keys. 'Don't worry. Go home. We'll sort it out and I'll be back in a few hours.'

'Don't bet on it,' Fitzwilliam said.

Greenacre had finally persuaded the police to let him through and he came bustling up, puce-faced with indignation. 'What the hell have you done to my office? I'll sue the lot of you.'

Wells took charge. 'You'll have to accompany us, sir. This is a very serious matter. A man's been badly hurt and property has been severely damaged. We'll need statements from everyone involved.'

Hank was holding Megan by the shoulders, half shielding her from the police. 'She's *not* involved!'

Wells nodded. 'You're free to go.'

Hank released her and Megan jiggled the keys. 'I don't know. I—'

'That's it,' Wells barked. 'We've stood around long enough for those TV bastards to get pictures and make up stories. Fitz, Carter, let's get moving.'

The cops herded us, and it was either fight or go. Megan understood and backed up.

'How's your fucking heart, Hardy?' Fitzwilliam whispered as we moved away from the TV lights and towards the cars.

'Cold as ice where you're concerned,' I said, 'and I'm considering just what recent conversations I might put in my statement.'

It would depress me to work in any institutional building, but the Surry Hills Police Centre would depress me more than most. The designers have done their best with the lighting and the pot plants, but the place carries an aura of bureaucratic and hierarchical insensitivity and fear. The junior cops fear their seniors, the senior cops fear the top brass, and they fear the politicians, lawyers and each other. Whenever I go in there, I get the sense that the police service doesn't have catching criminals at the top of its agenda.

Wells delegated a uniformed officer to put Hank and me together in one room and I saw Greenacre and Dimarco being ushered into separate rooms. In classical police style we were left alone for a spell. The room was comfortable enough, with carpet, institutional chairs and table, and an air-conditioner doing its thing. No windows; we were two floors below street level. Who ever heard of an interrogation room with a view?

'Reckon this place is bugged?' Hank said.

'You're the expert.'

He prowled the room. I tried to use my mobile but got no signal. Hank tried with the same result.

'I know why they didn't take the phones,' he said. 'I'm betting on a listening device of some sophistication.'

He raised his voice, 'Hear me, asshole?'

We sat in silence for a while before Hank said, 'I could do with a coffee.'

'Ask the guy with the earphones.'

Hank opened his mouth to shout again when Wells entered, or rather stood in the doorway.

'You can go,' he said.

I eased up out of the chair. It'd been a long night and, although I considered myself to be fully recovered, there was the odd creak and crack. 'Why's that?'

Wells smiled, well aware of what he was saying. 'Mr Dimarco's legal representative has made some strong representations.'

Hank waved his mobile. 'So you let him call out, while we were locked in the soundproof booth?'

'If you like,' Wells said. 'I'd suggest that a senior executive of an international firm ranks above a private detective like you with one strike against him, and another who's struck out. I think you follow me, Mr Bachelor.'

'Fuck you,' Hank said.

Wells swung away, leaving the door open. 'I liked *The Sopranos*, too,' he said. 'You forgot to add "cocksucker".'

* * *

Hank was a coffee addict and couldn't go much longer without a fix. We stopped at a Starbucks in Oxford Street.

If the barista was surprised to see a man with congealed blood spots on his face, she didn't react. Probably not unusual in Oxford Street. She took our orders and our money without a blink.

'Nice to have friends in high places,' Hank said.

'Hardly friends, but I reckon it rules out Global as the people who killed McKinley.'

'Leaving Lachlan and Tarelton. What's your bet, Cliff?'

We sat at a distance from the only other table occupied. The coffee arrived; I didn't really want it and I passed mine over to Hank after he'd drunk most of his, hot as it was, in a couple of gulps.

'Lachlan,' I said, 'on the follow-the-money principle. Dr O'Neil said Lachlan had lent money to Tarelton. That'd put Tarelton under pressure, but what if Lachlan had borrowed the money somewhere themselves? More pressure maybe. We know something about Global and Tarelton, but we know hardly anything about Lachlan.'

Hank moved on to the second mug. 'Megan was working on it but she didn't come up with anything that I know of. Hey, I should get home.'

'Me, too. I need to clean up these cuts and make sure I haven't got glass in my ears. How come you got away clean?'

'I hit the deck a mite faster than you, buddy.'

We walked, keeping an eye out for a cab. I was late for my evening meds and the thought annoyed me. How many times in rehab had they told me not to resent the fact that I had to take the medication for the rest of my life?

'Cliff,' Hank said when we'd almost reached Whitlam Square, 'I heard what you muttered to that asshole cop. What was all that about?'

'Tell you tomorrow. Here's a cab. What d'you reckon's closer—Glebe or Newtown?'

'Fifty-fifty.'

'Toss you for the fare.'

I won.

I cleaned up, took the pills and was about to go up to bed when I realised that I was wide awake with my mind buzzing. No chance of sleeping. I poured a scotch to replace the one I hadn't finished in Greenacre's office. I switched on the television and channel-hopped until I found a late news broadcast. The event in Double Bay got second billing. With the cameras kept at a distance and smoke in the night air, the shots of Hank, Dimarco and me weren't as clear as they might have been and the focus was initially on Holland being loaded into the ambulance and then on the firemen getting the troublesome electrical fires under control.

The cameras tracked Megan running towards us but Hank's bulk quickly shielded us all from the lens. The commentary accompanying the pictures had virtually no content, but that didn't stop the flow: 'This does not appear to be a terror-related incident, although that possibility has always to be borne in mind with several alleged terrorists facing trial and the well-known habit of terrorist organisations to . . .'

I was about to switch off when a camera caught an image of Phil Fitzwilliam and Sean Wells. Fitz was looking up at the shattered windows and his expression was close to one of satisfaction. Wells had missed this, but when Fitz stared appraisingly at Megan, Wells shot him a look of pure contempt.

19

Early the next morning, I phoned Megan's flat. Hank answered sleepily.

'It's Cliff. This is important. Don't let Megan out of your sight this morning. Don't let her go for the papers. Don't let her go for a swim. Don't let her do anything but stay with her till you get to the office. Can you secure the door to the street?'

'What? Yeah, once the other tenants are in. But that means no clients. Why . . .?'

'Before they get there, and we'll let them in one at a time. We'll just tell them it goes with the territory of sharing premises with a private eye. What time will you be there, precisely?'

Hank was alert now, sensing my seriousness. 'You name it.'

It was six twenty-five am, barely light. 'Eight o'clock sharp. I'll be there. I'll fill you in then.'

'You'd better do that, Cliff. You've been holding back on me . . . on us.'

I cut the call and took a big pull on the coffee I'd made to try to pep myself up after a minimal and restless sleep. My next call was to my oldest friend, Frank Parker, retired deputy commissioner of police but still with consultative roles of various kinds. He answered, only marginally less sleepy than Hank.

'Frank? Cliff Hardy.'

'Oh, Jesus, at this hour? I saw the news last night. What trouble are you in now?'

'Nothing special—bit of murder, intimidation, that sort of thing. I need some information about a certain long-serving, highly discreditable officer.'

'Are you on a secure line?'

'Is anyone these days?'

'True, well, I'll take a risk. That's the way it is with you, Cliff, right?'

'Keeps you young, Grandpa. Phil Fitzwilliam. I don't want details, just his current status.'

I knew that the police internal affairs unit kept a running check on officers who'd stepped over the line, whether they'd been brought to book or not. One of Frank's unofficial consultancies was with internal affairs. Frank had risen in the ranks through the tumultuous years of the New South Wales police service. Never mentioned in inquiries or Royal Commissions, he'd kept his nose clean through integrity and sheer intelligence—a rare combination in that world. He'd come close to disaster more than once when corrupt officers had tried to draw him in to their conspiracies. On one of these occasions, I'd been able to help him stay clear of the mess. Frank was grateful and loyal and he hated bent cops.

'Code red,' he said. 'Very compromised. Heading for a fall.'

'How hard a fall?'

'Professionally? Total.'

'Legally?'

'Hard to say. Possible he'd do some time. It'd depend on the quality of the lawyers he could afford.'

'What's the time frame?'

'Sooner rather than later. Be careful, Cliff. He's not just a money siphon, he's a vicious bastard and word is there are a couple of people under the dirt on his account. Not lately, but . . . Are you likely to cause him grief?'

'Maybe.'

'That'd be nice, but take care.'

I thanked him and rang off. Frank's son, Peter, was my anti-godson—all of us, Frank, his wife Hilde and me being staunch atheists. I'd taught Peter to surf until he was better at it than me. It was a close bond and Lily had been a part of it. I thought about her as I hung up. A freelance journalist, her pursuit of a story about police corruption had resulted in her murder. She'd have enjoyed a target like Phil Fitzwilliam.

I was at the door to the King Street building at a couple of minutes to eight and Hank, carrying a cardboard tray with three coffees on board, turned up on the dot with Megan.

'You look like you've been peppered with birdshot,' Hank said.

The cuts, now scabbing, made my face feel tight and sore. Smiling hurt, so I didn't smile. Hank looked tired, Megan looked worried; we weren't a happy bunch. I held the coffees while Hank unlocked the door, relocked it and kicked a wedge firmly into place.

'Unless things have changed we've got about an hour

undisturbed before the others get here,' I said. 'I've got a bit to tell you.'

I told them. About my longstanding enmity with Phil Fitzwilliam, about his approach and his threat to Hank's licence.

'You should have told me before,' Hank said.

'Yeah, but I thought it was bluff and . . .'

'You thought you could handle it yourself,' Megan said. 'Typical.'

'Something like that. Anyway, I spotted him again giving Margaret and me the eye and there he was again last night.'

Hank worked on his coffee, still antagonistic towards me. 'Doing what?'

'Being unpleasant, but I watched TV footage of the Double Bay stuff last night and I saw him taking a look at Megan. That worried me. Phil was notorious for getting to people through their family members. Applying pressure by proxy, sort of.'

'He can't pressure me,' Megan said. 'I haven't done anything since a bit of shoplifting when I was twelve. Oh, and one warning for dope possession.'

'You don't have to have done anything. Phil'd have access to cocaine, heroin, eccies—whatever you like, if he wanted to go that way.'

Megan still looked sceptical. 'Why would he?'

I finished my coffee. I'd already had some, strong and black, at home and now I was feeling a bit wired after no breakfast and God knows what chemicals in the pills I had to take. I could feel ideas jumping around in my head in no particular order and with no solid foundation. It must have showed.

'Are you all right, Cliff?' Megan said. 'Maybe we should leave this until—'

'Maybe we shouldn't,' Hank said.

I pulled myself together with an effort. 'Hank's right. I'm guessing now, trying to make connections, but Frank Parker tells me Fitzwilliam is in the gun with internal affairs. "Compromised", he said, and likely to need a lot of money for legal help to keep out of jail. I reckon he's in the pocket of whoever doesn't want an investigation of Henry McKinley's death.'

'Yeah,' Hank said, 'that plays, but who is it—Tarelton or Lachlan?'

I turned to Megan. 'What have you come up with on Lachlan?'

She shrugged. 'Very secretive. Ostensibly some kind of resources exploration outfit, but basically money movers. Registered in the Bahamas. A blog says they launder money, but it's a pretty hysterical blog. More sober sources say they're cashed-up, smallish, keen to grow.'

'Follow the money,' Hank said.

'I'm way out on a limb here now,' I said, 'but if I had to bet I'd like Lachlan for stopping the investigation and Tarelton for disrupting our meeting. My guess is that Tarelton still has hopes of getting through to the water, while Lachlan's worried about anyone finding out what happened to Dr Henry.'

'What about Lachlan's loan to Tarelton?' Hank said.

'It'd be small beer compared to what they'd face if they were convicted for arranging the murder of a prize-winning Australian scientist working for the common good.'

We sat around talking the thing over until a hammering on the street door broke up the meeting and Hank let the first of the other tenants in. I could hear him explaining things to the woman who ran a picture framing business and heard her laugh obligingly. Hank has a way about him.

'You said you had a casual working for you,' I said when Hank returned. 'The guy who nearly knocked me down the stairs. Apologised nicely but didn't introduce himself.'

'Ross Crimond. No, you're right. He hasn't been in touch for a time. There were signs he was in after hours the other night—he's got a key and the security code—but I'd have expected a report from him by now.'

'What's he working on?'

'Routine stuff—accident claims, process serving.'

'You say he was in at night. Does he have computer skills?'

'Of course—why I hired him.'

'Are you sure of him, Hank?'

Megan had let another tenant in and coming back she caught the tail end of our conversation.

'I'm not,' she said.

Hank looked uncomfortable. First, he'd learned that I'd held out on him, then that his lover could be targeted by a bad cop, now that she distrusted his professional judgement.

'Meg,' Hank said, 'he's OK.'

'He's a creep. A God-botherer. He wears polo shirts buttoned up to the neck and tucked into his pants.'

'You Ossies,' Hank snapped, 'any mention of God and you—'

'Hold it,' I said. 'Megan, can you find out whether this . . . what's his name again?'

'Ross Crimond,' Hank said.

'. . . whether he accessed your stuff on Tarelton, Lachlan and Global.'

'I think so.'

Worry replaced Hank's troubled look. 'He shouldn't do anything like that.'

Megan tapped away, swore, tapped some and then swung around. 'He's been into the files. He knows everything we know.'

'Maybe just curious,' Hank said.

Megan shook her head. 'He made copies.'

'Shit,' Hank said. 'I should have—'

'It's not so bad,' Megan said. 'He doesn't know anything about all this stuff Cliff keeps in his bloody head.'

Hank grinned, glad of her implied support, before he grabbed his mobile, dialled, waited.

'Turned off,' he said.

I said, 'Leave a message as if things are normal.'

Hank cleared his throat, 'Hey, Ross, waiting on that report. Check in soon, please.'

'What's on your mind, Cliff?' he said.

'Which company seems most likely to spend money getting at your employee and enlisting Phil Fitzwilliam?'

'Lachlan.' Hank and Megan said the word simultaneously.

'But,' Megan said, 'a couple of things trouble me. Why was Terry Dart killed and why didn't the Lachlan heavies search the Myall cottage?'

'I'm guessing,' I said, 'but they probably didn't intend to kill Dart. Probably just wanted to snatch him as they did McKinley and find out what he knew. It just went wrong. And whoever took McKinley probably had the brief to do that and nothing more. All up, you'd have to say they aren't very good at this sort of thing.'

'That's encouraging,' Hank said.

'The only way we're going to be able to flush them out is to let them think that we have the answer to the big questions—where the aquifer tapping sites are and the details of the technique. Also, just as important from their point of view, we know who killed McKinley.'

Hank nodded. 'Information we don't actually have.'

'I get it,' Megan said. 'Just suppose Crimond believes we *do* have that information, after he next digs into my files.'

'Trying not to be smug,' I said. 'But I have to say I see this as an opportunity.

20

The three of us put our heads together and concocted a story made up of fictitious interviews, the receipt of fictitious documents and aircraft flight plans. The upshot was that we were reporting to our client that we were in possession of information regarding police corruption and McKinley's discoveries. Megan entered all this into her files on the McKinley case.

Hank left Crimond another telephone message, delivered in a rushed manner, saying that the office would be closed for the afternoon and evening because he and Megan were going to take a joyride flight and then go to an important meeting. He said he hoped to see Crimond's report and expense sheet when he got in next morning.

We reviewed the material, revised it, criticised it.

'How bright is this guy?' I asked.

'Bright enough,' Hank said. 'I mean, efficient.'

Megan looked up from the keyboard. 'How bright is someone who believes the world was created six thousand years ago?'

'He's a creationist?' I said.

'Yup.'

'When does he think the world's going to end?'

'Dunno,' Megan said, 'but I'm sure he's got a view.'

'I still can't see why he'd cross the line,' Hank said, 'unless this bad cop of yours has him by the balls.'

'Could be that,' I said. 'Or money. Creationists aren't against money. Think of Oral Roberts.'

'The Hillsong Church,' Megan said.

Hank laughed. 'OK, you Darwinians. So we stake the place out and see if he takes the bait, right?'

We took turns watching from a cafe across the street at an angle to the office. Two-hour shifts, about as long as the waiters would tolerate someone sitting over two cups of coffee. Crimond arrived late in the afternoon on Hank's watch. Megan and I were nearby in her flat when Hank's call came. Meagan answered and handed me the phone.

'He's in,' Hank said. 'Been there a few minutes already. Wouldn't take that long to drop his stuff off.'

'Where's he parked?'

'He doesn't drive,' Megan said. 'He's an environmentalist. A green Christian.'

'Shit. If he's doing what we think he's doing, it'll seem urgent to him. How does he feel about taxis?'

'OK,' Hank said, 'judging from his expense sheets.'

Things in inner-west Sydney aren't the way they are in the movies. There are no taxis sitting, ready to follow other taxis. No spots for a car to idle, waiting to tail another car or a cab. It's a traffic jungle. We did the best we could while contributing to the pollution and the greenhouse effect: Megan and I got in our cars with our mobile phones and

cruised around the area, trying to cover the multiple directions our quarry might take if he caught a taxi.

Twenty minutes later Hank called my mobile. 'He's on
the move in a cab, heading towards the city. I'm fucked.
Had to sprint to my car but now I'm heading the other way
on King. He's stuck at the lights, but I'm just inching along,
no way to get round.'

I was out of it, too, going down Enmore Road. I phoned
Megan with the information. 'Where're you?'

'Yee-hah, I'm in King Street at the Missenden Road
lights and I see a taxi coming towards me in a little bunch
of other vehicles. Has to be him.'

Fine, I thought, *plan working, but why did it have to be
her?* A protective part of me wanted to ditch it, and part of
me didn't. I turned left, trying to snake my way back in the
right direction. I dived through a small gap, probably
causing road rage before I answered her.

'Follow him. We'll fall in behind and catch you as soon
as we can. Be careful, love. Be very careful.'

Megan and Hank had hands free communication in
their cars; I didn't, so I broke the law by staying in touch
with them on the mobile. Megan kept the taxi in sight and
kept up a running commentary as Hank and I tried to catch
up—difficult in the thick, late afternoon traffic. Megan was
enjoying herself. That worried me.

I was reminded of the John Cleese commercial for golf
balls where he said in mock Scots: 'It's a Scottish game—it
was no meant to be fun.' This business wasn't meant to be
fun, but I'd be lying if I said it wasn't. The thing is, it isn't
always fun, and Megan had yet to find that out. She'd
kicked a would-be arsonist downstairs and now she was
following a taxi like Bogart in *The Maltese Falcon*. High

points; the low points would come. I didn't want them to. I didn't want her in the business. I didn't want the responsibility.

I wrestled with these thoughts as I tracked Megan over the Harbour Bridge. Hank passed me, let me know he was doing it, and I had conflicting thoughts about him, too: *Hiring a creationist? Critical of us sceptics?*

Hank called me. 'Got her in sight, looks to be headed towards Manly.'

He hung up and Megan called. 'Manly,' she said, 'and guess whose headquarters are in Manly? Lachlan Enterprises. The cab's heading that way—see you there, and don't even say it, Cliff—I won't let him spot me.'

'Cruise past,' I said. 'Stop as near as you can where you can't be seen and point it out to us.'

We met up in a street beside Ivanhoe Park. Megan pointed across to an office building that went up about as high as regulations allowed in the area.

'Pretty good taxi ride,' I said. 'Wonder if he'll put it on his expense sheet.'

'He better not,' Hank said grimly, 'the son of a bitch. That was great work, Meg, keeping the cab in sight all that way.'

'It's in the genes,' I said.

We stood, looking across at the building in the fading light. The breeze from the water did the things it always does in Sydney—lifted the spirits, whetted the appetite and the thirst.

'They're up there chewing over the bogus information,' Megan said. 'So important that he had to do it in person, not with a phone call. The question is, who in the Lachlan mob is in the game?'

'The dirty work'd be contracted out,' I said, 'but someone inside Lachlan'd be handling the operation.'

'I can get a list of the principals,' Megan said.

Hank stretched to his full 195 centimetre height; the muscles in his back and shoulders pushed his jacket up and the sleeves were stretched tight by his biceps and triceps and other muscles most of us don't have or know about. 'Fuck that,' he said. 'We need to have a meeting with Ross.'

I could feel tension building between the pair and didn't want it to go any higher. 'It's a nice night,' I said, 'and we're in magnificent Manly. I vote we talk about it over a few drinks and something to eat.'

'Your solution for just about everything,' Megan said.

Not a great start.

We found a fish restaurant near the water. If there's a better meal than grilled barramundi with chips and salad and dry white wine I don't know what it is. We all opted for the same thing—the beginning, I hoped, of restored harmony. The first few glasses would help, too.

'I'll be the mug,' Megan said when she'd demolished half of her meal. 'What say we assemble everything we have and turn it over to the police. They grill Ross-baby, investigate Lachlan and like that.'

I shook my head. 'We haven't got enough on Crimond. A good lawyer'd give him protection and probably threaten Hank with a suit for something—slander, unfair dismissal.'

Hank nodded. 'The cops probably wouldn't touch it. It's all too . . . loose.'

Megan speared a chip. 'So?'

Hank said, 'I vote we put the pressure on Ross to name names.'

Megan looked doubtful; she nibbled at an impaled chip. 'Threatening him with what? Violence?'

Hank shrugged.

I'd been digesting what we knew as well as the good food. I had a clean plate and an empty glass. I grabbed the wine bottle and poured the last of it—a small measure for each of us. It was the second bottle. We'd need coffee and a walk before taking to our cars.

'We've established the connection,' I said. 'Good first step. Now we have to hook them firmly and get them to show their hand.'

'How?' Megan said.

'By convincing them that we know, or are close to knowing, what McKinley discovered and that we've got a lead on who killed him.'

'You said that. I still say how?'

'I'm open to suggestions.'

'Don't be coy, Cliff,' Hank said. 'What've you got in mind?'

'We have to draw someone, anyone'll do, from Lachlan out into the open. We're pretty sure McKinley was picked up in Myall. We've got the evidence, the specs. What if we've discovered a witness?'

Hank and Megan exchanged looks. 'You cunning bastard,' Hank said.

I nodded. 'Thank you. I'm not saying it'll work, but we've identified what they believe to be a mole—sorry for the spook-talk—inside our operation. We've already fed him some disinformation. We can feed him some more—like a meeting we're arranging somewhere with a fictitious witness.'

Hank signalled for the waiter and ordered three long black coffees. 'They'd want their hard guy, the contractor, there for a meeting like that.'

I drank the last of my wine. 'I would.'

'A fictitious witness,' Megan said. 'Jesus, we'll need to be inventive.'

'Jesus could just be the key,' I said.

21

I was introduced to Ross Crimond in Hank's office the next day. He'd come in, he said, to discuss the report and expense sheet he'd dropped in the night before, but it was clear he was looking to hang around, hoping to pick up additional bits of information. He was thirtyish, fair, freckled, stocky. He was one of those people that the loosening up of dress, language and manners that had started in the sixties seemed to have passed by. He wore neat trousers, shirt and tie and a jacket. His shoes had been polished recently. Nerdy, you'd call him, until you saw the body language and heard him talk. He spoke in a deep confident voice and moved like a dancer. Hank had told me that he had a business and criminology degree from Bond University and had won medals as a fencer. He'd passed the TAFE PEA course with flying colours and done a few yards as an insurance investigator.

His handshake was firm and I remembered his steadying hand on the stairs. 'Mr Hardy,' he said, 'heard a lot about you. Glad to meet you. Goodness, it was you on the stairs.'

'Cliff,' I said. 'No harm done.'

'You lectured at the Petersham TAFE a few years before I got there.'

'Hardly that,' I said. 'I gave a few talks—brought in a few cops and crims as props.'

'You were a legend.'

I shrugged. 'You seem to have all the right tickets, Ross. If you don't mind me asking, why're you slumming as a casual in this crummy outfit?'

A strike against him right there—no sense of humour. He took a beat or two to reply and said, 'I intended to make this my profession, but quite recently I received the Lord Jesus Christ into my life and now I'm in training to be a minister in the Soul Saviour Church.'

'Good luck,' I said. 'Costs money does it, the training?'

'Not that much, but the more one can contribute to the congregation the better one prays, and performs at everything.'

'That's what's wanted, performance,' I said. 'Hey, Hank, how was the joy flight? Did you find McKinley's pilot?'

Hank looked up from his computer. 'Working on it.'

Crimond smiled. 'Joy flight. That sounds nice. Business or pleasure?'

'Business,' Hank said. 'We've got this case—dead geologist looking for something worth a zillion. We got a tip he was looking from the air. We're trying to find the pilot who took him up. I've got a licence myself. Went for a spin with Meg yesterday just to get familiarised at the airport. Could be a long haul. This report's fine, Ross, and the expenses are on the light side. You could spread yourself a bit more.'

'Can I help with this case you've got?'

'Maybe,' Hank said. 'Come in here and we'll talk about it.'

Megan went on with her work at the computer and I took myself off to the gym. I'd neglected my workouts for a few days, and I felt the effects of the lay-off when I got on the first machine. There are two schools of thought in this situation: one says push through it at the level you're used to, and the other says take it a bit easier. I go with the latter. Wesley Scott wandered out of his office and watched me on the seated rower.

'Haven't seen you lately, man.'

I tried not to sound short of breath when I answered but I couldn't help it. 'Busy.'

'Cemetery's full of busy men not so busy now.'

'You're a ray of sunshine, Wes.'

'I like to remind people that an hour and a dollar spent here saves money on your hospital bills. You're doing OK, Cliff. Just don't slack off. Let's see another set.'

Back in the office I found Crimond gone, Megan off for a swim, and Hank looking pleased with himself.

'How'd it go?' I asked.

'I think he bought it. I went with your suggestion— told him we might possibly have a witness to McKinley being taken away, but we weren't sure. I said the party was a very religious person and you and Megan, as unbelievers, weren't sure of his sanity.'

'That's good,' I said. 'You were extemporising there, mate.'

'Sure. I said we were trying to line up a meeting with him and a person from his church and that maybe Ross could be useful at the meeting.'

'He lapped it up?'

'He's not dumb, Cliff. Don't make that mistake now that he's a player. He questioned me a bit and I fed him some stuff about the spectacles that helped to convince him. I mentioned the village. As I say, I think he went for it.'

'Good. Sounds as if you handled it just right.'

'So now we set up a meeting with the imaginary witness, with Ross invited along, and he tells Lachlan and they send someone. We grab that someone and pressure him and Ross and . . . what can go wrong?'

'Everything,' I said.

'You're mad,' Megan said when we outlined the plan. 'You mean you intend to trot along to some dodgy meeting and confront the person, or persons, who killed Henry McKinley and torched his body?'

'Not without back-up,' I said.

'The police?'

'Not yet.'

Megan was right; it was time to stop going it alone. I was about to explain the next part of the plan when my mobile rang.

'Mr Hardy, this is Susan O'Neil.'

'Yes, Dr O'Neil.'

'I handed in my notice at Tarelton. They reacted furiously and threatened to sue me for breaking my contract, which isn't true, strictly speaking. I was wrestling with that when I got a call from Lachlan Enterprises offering me a job at a higher salary with better conditions. I mentioned the difficulty I was having with Tarelton and they offered to meet any legal costs I might incur. What's going on? It's all about Henry, isn't it? I feel I'm caught in the middle of something I don't understand, and my professional reputation is a sort of football.'

'You're exactly right,' I said, 'but we think things are coming together. My advice is to keep your head down for a time. Say, a week. Can you do that?'

She said she could and I told her I'd keep her in touch with developments.

'You're juggling a few balls, you two,' Megan said.

I nodded. 'Quite a few and more to come.'

Hank and I had discussed the next move. He called Dimarco at Global Resources and gave him an outline of how things stood—our belief that Lachlan Enterprises was behind McKinley's death and our confidence that Global wasn't involved.

The conversation was on broadcast: 'Thanks for the vote of confidence,' Dimarco said. 'And what about the results of Dr McKinley's research?'

'That's still uncertain.'

Megan raised an eyebrow.

Dimarco said, 'Well, that's very interesting but why're you talking to me?'

'Your rivals,' Hank said, 'in this and I'd guess other things, are Tarelton and Lachlan. Tarelton's in financial trouble, borrowing money, losing staff. Lachlan lent them money and are worried about getting it back, let alone a return. They're trying to poach Tarelton's people. We have a scheme to prove their involvement in McKinley's death. That'd be devastating for them, good for you.'

'I can see that,' Dimarco said. 'But I still don't see—'

'We need your help.'

Hank told Dimarco in very general terms about our entrapment plans. He said that when the meeting took place we'd need him present as a witness and the help of some of Global's security people. You can't go wrong appealing to the ego of corporations and their executives. There was a distinctly eager note in Dimarco's voice when he said he'd discuss the proposition with CEO Holland.

'How's he doing?' Hank asked.

'He's healing, but he's angry. I think we can do business.'

Hank told him he'd be in touch about the meeting and they could make strategic plans.

When he'd finished the call, Megan turned to her computer and began scrolling through files.

'Hah,' she said, 'according to these notes, Hank, you reckoned that Dimarco and this copper Wells were seeing eye to eye. Dimarco'll tell him all about this.'

'He will,' I said, 'when we're ready for him to do just that.'

We agreed to set up the meeting for two nights ahead at my house. There were plenty of places for our back-up team to hide themselves—upstairs, in the jungle of vine and creeper at the side of the place and at the back of the block where it dipped down sharply and there were neglected and over-grown bushes.

'A homey atmosphere,' I said, 'makes for confidence.'

'It'll take careful orchestrating—choreographing, really,' Megan said. 'The Lachlan people'll want to see a real witness.'

'Any suggestions?'

'Ross knows all of us,' Hank said. 'We need a cleanskin.'

'Patrick,' Megan said. 'He'd be perfect, and he'd jump at the chance.'

'I bet he would,' Hank said.

Patrick Fox-James was an actor and musician. He and

Megan had been on together for a few years; they'd performed in plays and done a two-hander comedy act on a Pacific cruise boat. The relationship had fizzled out. I never knew why. Hank's jealousy was understandable. Actors—you could never tell about them. But Megan was right; Fox-James could play the part and the danger involved wouldn't deter him. He'd done his own stunts in some television work. He looked like an aesthete, but was physically tough and courageous. We persuaded Hank.

We left it there for the time being. As Megan said, it was going to be tricky: we had to draw Crimond in and give him time to contact the players at Lachlan; we had to work on Dimarco, anticipate his moves, and eventually agree to allow a police presence. Choreography.

I left Hank and Megan not on the very best of terms. As Bob Dylan says, 'How much do we have to pay for going through these things twice?' Or more than twice. Relationships have their own dynamic and agendas and you intervene at your peril.

I walked home. King Street was buzzing and would buzz until the early hours. The evening was cool and I kept up a brisk pace going through Victoria Park to the Glebe Point Road intersection. Glebe at night used to be more like Newtown, busier than it was now. Gentrification had quietened it down. I bought some Lebanese takeaway and cleanskin white wine and prepared for another lonely night. I was in a strange mood as I made my way down towards the water: I missed Lily but my thoughts turned quite often to Margaret McKinley; I was working again, but not really working, not in the old way.

I reached my gate and juggled the food and wine as I scrabbled for my keys. I heard a sound, caught a smell, then felt a stabbing pain in the small of my back. *A kidney punch!* I dropped everything and turned to hit back but a blow to the side of my head blurred my vision. Another blow blacked me out. Funny things happen in moments like that—all I registered as the darkness closed in was that the wine bottle hadn't broken.

22

When I came to, I found myself in my own living room, with a plastic restraint anchoring my right wrist to the arm of the sofa. A damp towel hit me in the face.

'Fix yourself up a bit, Hardy. You're a mess.'

The voice was familiar, but my vision was still fuzzy. I used the wet towel to clear my eyes and then pressed it against the aching places on my head. A lighter clicked and I smelled tobacco and smoke. Phil Fitzwilliam lounged against the wall near where I sat. He drew on his cigarette and flicked ash on the carpet.

'I warned you, Hardy.'

The cool towel felt good against the throbbing spots. I blinked several times and began to feel as if I might be able to talk and function. I'd been wrong about Fitz: a direct approach; not one of his sideways jobs as in the past. What did that mean? Confidence? Desperation?

'You're out on a long, thin limb here, Phil.'

'I wouldn't say that.'

He took a ballpoint pen from the breast pocket of his jacket, reached into another pocket and fished out a pistol.

He wiped the pistol with a handkerchief and put the pen up the barrel. He opened the door of the cupboard under the stairs and shoved the pistol deep into the jumble inside. Then he shut the door and opened it, feigning surprise.

'What's this? Looks like an illegal weapon, traceable to a serious wounding, with your fingerprints on it. With your record . . .'

'What about the coke and the paedophiliac porn?'

'No need. I can guarantee you some time inside, Hardy, and you and I know there are people in there who'll be pleased to see you.'

'They'll be more pleased to see you when your time comes.'

He smiled. 'Never happen.'

The ash on his cigarette was long now. He reached to the nearest bookshelf, turned the photograph of Lily over, and carefully deposited the ash on top of it.

'That cunt got what she deserved.'

I shook my head, even though it hurt. 'Phil, Phil, you're a worried man. Internal affairs are breathing down your neck. You say I've got enemies in jail—you've got 'em inside and outside. I'd say that Sean Wells'd like to see you in the protection unit at the Bay. Probably wouldn't visit except to see how stressed you were.'

'All manageable.'

'Yeah, maybe. With money. How much is Tarelton paying you to run interference?'

'Who says anyone's paying me? Maybe I just hate your guts.'

'You never did anything on impulse, Phil. There was always a quid in it for you. And we're talking about a big quid here. D'you know about this water thing?'

Fitzwilliam was never hard to read. Until I used the magic word, he was getting ready to drop his butt on the carpet and stamp it out, but he changed his mind. He lifted his foot, stubbed the cigarette on his heel and dropped the butt on the upturned photograph.

'What about water?'

'They're keeping you in the dark, mate. A guy named McKinley was working for Tarelton. He discovered a way to solve the city's water problem forever and a day. Then he got killed, as you'd know. Hank and I were investigating the murder for McKinley's daughter. Tarelton became uneasy, made some funny moves we caught on to. They wanted to stop our investigation and see if some way could still be found to turn on the tap, if you follow me. What did they tell you? Let me guess. They said we were looking for evidence to back the daughter's duty of care suit and that they were facing a big payout and needed your help. That's bullshit.'

'Fuck you. You always talked a blue streak, Hardy, and got yourself out of trouble. Not this time.'

But I knew I'd got to him. At his best, Fitzwilliam was quietly menacing, but it could turn to bluster when he lost confidence. I'd seen it before in the witness box, and it was obvious again now.

'Tarelton's in trouble,' I said. 'There're two other players in the game. Tarelton borrowed big money from one of them and is under pressure. These three are all still hoping to get in on the water deal. Tarelton's got at least one shadow minister on side and the others've probably done the same. It's state and federal politics and international capitalism, Phil. Too big for you, too big for us, but we can still get something out of it if we play it smart.'

Fitzwilliam lit another cigarette. 'You've just about lost me, but go on.'

'There's some guesswork in it from us, but it looks like this: Tarelton hired a shooter to break up the meeting between Hank and me and Global Enterprises—that's one of the other players. The shots were aimed high—no real risk to life or limb. The guy from Global copped some flying glass. I suspect you arranged that, but . . . never mind.'

'The fuck do you mean, never mind?'

'We think the other player was responsible for McKinley's death and probably another one. That's who we're after.'

'A couple of cowboys, that's what you two are. Even if I believed this bullshit you'd never stand a chance against these big companies. They've got money to burn and more lawyers than you can shake a stick at.'

I shrugged. 'Have it your own way. In any case, we're not interested in Tarelton. There's no reason for you to put the moves on us.'

'Like I say, maybe I just want to.'

'Look, Phil, you can do yourself some good out of this. Pick up some points you're going to need when internal affairs come down on you.'

'Who says they will?'

'I have my sources.'

'Fucking Parker.'

Just the mention of the name seemed to bring the trouble hanging over him closer to his mind. He dropped more ash on the floor.

'For Christ's sake go out to the kitchen and get a bloody ashtray. I'm not going anywhere.'

He did, returning with another cigarette alight and a saucer. He had a decent slug of my whisky in a glass. He settled into a chair and stared at me. He sipped, crossed his legs, trying for casual and not making it.

'Go on,' he said, 'entertain me.'

'You know how it works. It's tit for tat. If you were in on a successful murder prosecution—exposing corporate corruption, protecting the public interest—a lot of your transgressions would be downgraded, even forgiven. It'd be worth a whole lot more to you than putting a couple of private eyes out of business.'

'I'm listening.'

'I don't like you any more than you like me, but I've got a proposition for you, Phil.'

23

'He's coming down tomorrow morning,' Hank said to Ross Crimond. 'We're going to put him up in Cliff's place.'

'Why?'

'He's got the room.'

'I've got space. From what you said, he might be more comfortable in a Christian home—no offence, Mr Hardy.'

I wanted to hit him, but I said, 'He's more concerned about security than anything else. He knows what he's doing is dangerous. Hank and I can take shifts.'

Crimond was in a difficult spot. He didn't want to seem to be too aware of the dangers, but he wanted to get things arranged in his, or Lachlan's, favour. I could see his mind working.

'Danger?' he said. 'I don't quite follow.'

'Don't go there,' Hank said. 'But we'd like you to be present when we grill . . . talk to him. We need a rock solid statement of interview to take to . . . wherever we take it.'

Crimond nodded. 'Understood. So it's a meeting at Mr Hardy's place tomorrow at . . .?'

'Keep your mobile charged,' Hank said. 'Time to be

advised. And thanks, Ross, I reckon you'll be able to help us gain his confidence.'

Crimond gave a thin smile. 'Because I'm a sobersides?'

'Haven't heard that expression in years,' I said.

We started juggling the balls the following morning. Hank rang Dimarco and told him that if he presented at a time to be advised at my house the following night, he'd learn something to his advantage. Hank also said it'd be a good idea to bring a couple of his security people along.

The phone was on broadcast for my benefit.

'This involves Dr McKinley?'

'Sure does, and that's all I can tell you.'

'I'll think about it,' Dimarco said.

'Bet your ass you will,' Hank said after the call finished.

Then we got a surprise. About an hour after the call to Dimarco, the door buzzer sounded. Megan, research assistant-cum-receptionist, was away coaching Patrick Fox-James. I opened the door and stepped back in surprise.

'Hello, Mr Hardy,' the woman said, holding up her warrant card. 'Remember me? DS Roberts?'

'I do. Come in.'

She moved past me, put her card away in her bag and spun around. 'I'm here under instruction from Chief Super Dickersen whom I'm sure you also remember.'

Hank came out of his office. 'We remember him,' he said.

'I'm here to talk, and if the talk isn't satisfactory, to arrest you both for obstructing the course of justice, and conspiracy to commit a crime of violence.'

'Why didn't the chief super come himself?' I said.

'He was too busy and too angry. Just not sure you were worth his time. Can we get down to it?'

The wires or the satellite or both had been doing their thing. As we expected, Dimarco had contacted Wells. There was so much competitiveness within the police service that I'd expected Wells to take a personal interest and make the running himself. He'd have had the rationalisation that the Double Bay shooting was his case. But I'd been mistaken. Wells had contacted Chief Superintendent Dickersen who was overseeing the McKinley investigation—hence the presence of DS Roberts.

We had no choice. We gave her the outline of our plan—minus the time and place of the crucial meeting—to flush out the people responsible for Henry McKinley's death. She listened with scepticism and impatience written all over her. The impatience was understandable—she'd have got most of this from Wells. The scepticism made sense, too. As we laid it out for the fourth time (counting the versions to Megan, Crimond and Dimarco), it began to sound less and less feasible. That's the way it is with plans. The best chance for their success is to state them once and carry them out.

DS Angela Roberts, crisp and comfortable in her light-weight suit, now wore an expression you'd have to call amused. 'That would be the dopiest idea I've heard in a long time,' she said. 'How could you hope to pull it off?'

'There's a lot of dopiness about this case, Detective,' I said. 'We've got three big companies all angling for this information that they'll probably never get. All with a mind to screw the public for profit. Two of them prepared to resort to violence, and one looks to have gone too far with it.'

She nodded. Didn't speak.

I went on, 'You know what it's like, with their lawyers and commercial confidentialities shields. They're hard to penetrate by conventional methods. Our client wants to know who's accountable. We can't see any other approach than the direct one.'

'You're involving people who aren't accountable—your stand-in witness and your employee, Mr Bachelor, who you've more or less entrapped.'

'It's messy,' Hank said.

'It just got more messy. You were counting on back-up from Global and Inspector Wells. Where are you now on that?'

Hank put his hands on the desk. They were big, powerful hands, but the way he placed them indicated his professional impotence. 'I guess we'll have to do some rethinking,' he said.

I hadn't mentioned Phil Fitzwilliam's second coming to Hank or Megan, out of a long habit of keeping tricky things to myself. That made it loom as even more tricky. To reveal it at this point would surely increase DS Roberts's doubts. She'd been taking notes as we spoke. Now she tapped her pen against her big white teeth.

'And where and when is this bloody gunfight at the OK corral going to take place?'

Hank and I exchanged glances before Hank shook his head. 'I'm afraid we're not at liberty to reveal that.'

'I said I could arrest you.'

'The meeting'd still go ahead,' I said. 'Just that our side would be undermanned.'

'You're bluffing.'

I shrugged. 'If you say so. Why don't you put it to Ian Dickersen that he's got a chance to close out a high profile murder case and drop some corporate creeps in the shit.'

'Ian's not a big noter.'

'You don't get to his level without making a name for yourself,' I said. 'And there're always more steps to take.'

She chewed that over, and she wouldn't have been human if she hadn't been thinking about her own part in the scheme of things. She closed her notebook and tucked it into a smart black leather bag that had a discreet Aboriginal flag medallion attached.

'I'll report to him and we'll be in touch.'

'Make it soon,' I said.

'You know what your great talent is, Mr Hardy?'

'*I'd* like to know,' Hank said.

She stood, ready to go. 'Almost, but not quite, pissing people off.'

Good exit line and she took it.

Hank was grinning and I gave him the bird. 'What she means is, my style leaves space for charm.'

So it was a waiting game—us waiting for Dickersen; Crimond waiting for us; Lachlan waiting for Crimond; Patrick Fox-James waiting for Megan; Phil Fitzwilliam waiting for me. In all this I'd almost forgotten about Margaret and I wasn't ready for her call at home that night.

'Cliff, this is Margaret. Please pick up if you're there.'

I hesitated and I wasn't sure why. I didn't know anymore whether the relationship was professional or personal or a mixture of both. Confusing. While I hesitated, I had a flash of us making love in the motel. Over the years, so many motels, and a few of them, with similar scenes playing out. Mostly signifying nothing. I grabbed the phone.

'Margaret.'

'Cliff.'

There was a pause and then she laughed. 'What is this, a scene from Noël Coward?'

I laughed, too. 'I was deep in thought.'

'About me?'

'And other matters.'

'You know that old joke about the girl who falls in love with the gorilla, but he doesn't call, he doesn't write. These days you could add—he doesn't email, he doesn't text.'

'I'm sorry. A lot has been happening, some of it good, some not so good. I was holding off until we had a result.'

'Are you close to that?'

'We could be, but it might all still go wrong.'

'Well, I'll leave that to you and Hank and Megan, but I was really calling about . . . us. I miss you.'

A statement like that should warm the heart, but it caught me on the hop. With a string of failed relationships behind me I was never confident the next time at bat. My wife Cyn had provided the diagnosis long ago. 'You live in your head, Cliff,' she said, 'with your clients and victims and perps. Everyone else just flits in and out.' It hadn't been a problem with Lily, possibly because we both did the same thing, but it had brought things unstuck in the past. It was time to snap out of it, if I could.

'Margaret,' I said, 'don't give up on me.'

'Give me something not to give up on.'

I tried. I talked. I gave her a version of where things stood with the investigation, but I could tell that wasn't what she was asking. I knew I was deliberately misinterpreting what she said. I suspect she knew it as well. I had a sense that she was involved in some kind of decision process, involving me, perhaps, but without telling me the terms. It all made for a very unsatisfactory phone conversation.

24

DS Roberts rang the next morning to say that Dickersen had agreed to go along with our plan with several non-negotiable provisos: Roberts herself and another officer were to be given several hours' notice of the venue and time of the meeting. They were empowered to inspect the meeting place and to cancel the event if they thought it unsatisfactory. They were empowered to intervene at any point they chose.

'What if we don't agree?' Hank said.

'Then you and Mr Hardy will be proceeded against on various charges relating to violation of the Private Enquiry Agents Act and withholding information from the police in respect of several serious crimes.'

'Several?' Hank said.

'The shooting at Double Bay and the death of Henry McKinley.'

'We don't have any hard evidence on the shooting.'

'Hard or soft, you haven't told us everything you know.'

'The same might go for you.'

'We're the authorities, you're not.'

'You win,' Hank said. 'We should know where and when by early afternoon. Who do we contact?'

'Who d'you think?' she said.

We waited a few hours and then started phoning. I told DS Roberts the meeting was set for seven thirty and that I'd meet her and her colleague at my house at five. Hank phoned Ross Crimond and told him the time and place—giving him a few hours to contact the Lachlan people. I phoned Megan with the information and arranged for her and Fox-James to meet us in the office for a briefing.

That left me with the problem of Phil Fitzwilliam and nobody to consult with on the matter. Well, that wasn't unusual. I went for a walk to Australia Park, sat under a tree and thought, but nothing inspirational came. Trees and grass and fresh air are overrated. No other course but the standard Hardy one—the direct approach. I phoned him.

'About fuckin' time,' he said.

'Don't be like that, Phil. I'm trying to do you a favour.'

'Trying to save your arse, more like.'

'That, too. Sorry, but there've been developments.'

I told him about Roberts and Dickersen and the way things stood.

'Jesus, Hardy, you're a lying, sneaky cunt.'

'Takes one to know one. You can still get something out of this. All you have to do is be there, behave like a policeman, and share in the glory.'

'With Ian fuckin' Dickersen and everyone's pet boong?'

'He's going up. Play your part and you might get him onside for your upcoming trouble.'

'I'll tell you this. If it doesn't work out in my fuckin' favour you and everyone connected with you is going to wish they'd never been born. That's a promise.'

So now I had threats from the police in two directions—not a record, but up there with some of my better
efforts. I told him where to go and when.

I got back to the office just as Megan and Fox-James
arrived. He was a slim, fair individual, something like the
old movie actor Leslie Howard in appearance. When
Megan had suggested him she'd told me in private why the
affair hadn't lasted long.

'Too tortured,' she said.

Whatever that meant. I reflected that it was good news
for Hank. No way could anyone brand Hank Bachelor as
tortured.

'Gidday, Cliff,' Fox-James said. 'I hear you had heart
trouble.'

'Thing of the past, Paddy. Ready to go into your act?
I see you've dressed for the part.'

He was wearing brown polyester slacks, black shoes and
a fawn polo shirt buttoned up to the neck. He looked like
a grown-up little boy dressed by his mother.

'Great threads, eh? What does the good book say? "Let
not thy raiment speak too loud".'

'Don't overdo it,' I said.

'You made that up,' Megan hissed. 'This is serious.'

'You were always telling me I was *too* serious.'

'There's a time and a place, Patrick. We have to talk to
Hank.'

Our meeting was anything but easy. Hank was jealous
of Fox-James, Fox-James resented Hank, Megan hated
being the meat in the sandwich, and I was still worrying
about Phil Fitzwilliam. But then, they say Clay was almost
hysterical with anxiety before the first Liston fight and look
what happened there.

I got to my place at four thirty and found Roberts and her colleague parked in the street more or less as I expected, and Fitz parked a few cars back. All three police officers, Roberts's colleague as dark as herself, followed me into the house. Roberts was fuming.

'What's he doing here?' she said, barely acknowledging Fitz.

'We have a history,' I said. 'As I explained to DS Fitz-william, this is a complicated matter. He has a piece of it, as the sports managers say.'

Fitz grinned at that; Roberts didn't. 'Don't come the smartarse sporting chat with me, Hardy. This farce is over.'

I had nothing to lose. I got right in her face, elbowing the other cop aside. 'No, it isn't. Let me tell you what's going to happen here, with a bit of luck. A couple of heavies from Lachlan Enterprises—courtesy of Ross Crimond, who's a deluded, ambitious hypocrite along the lines of the late, unlamented Joh Bjelke-Petersen—are going to show up with a company executive. A person claiming to be a witness to the abduction of Henry McKinley will be present. He'll represent himself as someone willing to overlook what he saw in return for a reward that will further the work of the Lord. The executive will haggle with the price. The witness will turn bolshie and the heavies will threaten and attempt to assault him. All this will be captured on videotape.'

Roberts rolled her eyes. 'Then what?'

'Then you and your mate and DS Fitzwilliam step in and arrest the heavies and the executive, take them away and work on them until someone cracks and drops the other, or others, in the shit.'

'I like it,' Fitz said.

'You would,' Roberts snarled. 'It's just your bullshit style.'

'Fuck you,' Fitz said.

'You wish.'

'Stop it,' I said. 'We haven't got much time. I admit it's as speculative and shaky as things get. But is there any other way to get at Henry McKinley's killers? Fitz needs the brownie points and you and your boss Dickersen want to climb the greasy pole. It's just a sting. You people have done them before.'

The other cop spoke for the first time. 'Detective Constable John Mahoud, Mr Hardy,' he said. 'What if it all goes wrong?'

Good question, I thought. 'I'll take the blame,' I said.

The police went upstairs while I set up the camcorder. Megan arrived with Hank and Fox-James and I installed them in the living room. The doorbell rang.

'Crimond,' Hank said. 'If he's on his own we're fucked.'

I let him in. He wasn't on his own. He had two men with him, both wearing suits and serious expressions. The older one was fleshy with a high colour; the other man was lean and hard looking. His glance swept the room and the people in it like a searchlight.

Ex-military, I thought. *Dangerous.*

Crimond was all smarm. 'This is Deacon Jones and Pastor Sorenson from my church,' he said. 'Deacon Jones is also . . .'

'An executive at Lachlan Enterprises,' I said.

Crimond didn't miss a beat. 'Why, yes.' He held out two hands to Fox-James. 'Ross Crimond.'

Fox-James was up to it. He gripped both hands and beamed. 'Piers Beaumont.'

Megan patted Fox-James on the head and moved away. I used a foot switch under the rug to activate the silent camcorder. Jones settled himself in a chair; Sorenson leaned against the cupboard under the stairs.

Hank got to his feet and loomed over Crimond. 'What's this, Ross? We just wanted you here to make Piers feel more at home when he told us about . . . well, you know.'

Crimond now showed his true colours. He couldn't help the contempt creeping into his voice as he looked briefly at me then focused on Hank.

'You're out of your depth, Bachelor. There are big things at stake here—for New South Wales, of course, but more importantly for a godly society.'

Fox-James's expression was one of puzzled idiocy. 'Amen,' he said.

Sorenson was looking from Hank to me, weighing us up. He didn't seem too worried. Jones leaned forward in his chair. 'You may not realise it, Mr Beaumont, but the decision you make here can affect—'

Fox-James visibly shrivelled where he sat. 'I don't understand.'

'You don't have to bear witness to anything. If you leave these godless people this minute, I can assure you of a reward that—'

Patrick Fox-James had been well briefed and his glance at me, and my nod, took a micro-second. He showed he had guts to spare as he rose from the chair, pointed at Sorenson, and screamed, 'I saw that man—'

Sorenson was on the move and so was I. He stepped

sideways and a pistol appeared in his hand. Shouts and noises on the stairs distracted him momentarily as he fitted a silencer to the muzzle. Fox-James hit the ground and rolled. I acted without thinking, as if no thought was necessary: I jerked the door under the stairs open and grabbed the pistol Fitzwilliam had left there. It was a Smith & Wesson .38 revolver that felt as familiar as my toothbrush. I swung it on Sorenson who was manoeuvring for a shot at Fox-James, and the instruction of decades before travelled through my brain: *Don't aim, point and fire.*

Well-trained, Sorenson registered me as a threat. He swivelled and the black hole of his silencer gaped at me. I pointed and fired, but so did he.

25

On the flight back from the States I'd seen a not-very-good film, *The Black Dahlia.* In an early scene, two men are talking about a woman who is standing between them. She says, 'Keep talking about me in the third person—it sends me.'

It didn't send me, but that's how I felt sometimes during my long stay in hospital. Sorensen's bullet had bounced around inside me, nicking various organs, and the wounds had become infected. They put me in an induced coma for a while and I lapsed into comas all of my own making a few times later.

Coming out of the fogs before dipping back into them again, I heard things like: *I think he'll pull through/He's got a raging infection/He's very weak/ He's fighting hard/His age is against him/He's got an amazing basic constitution . . .*

When the mist finally cleared and the pain cut in as they lowered the doses of whatever they were pumping into me, the day came when I was able to recognise Megan and Hank and smell the flowers Margaret had ordered for me.

'Hey, Dad,' Megan said.

Sounds weird, but I felt tears welling when I heard that.

'I refuse to say where am I,' I said. I didn't recognise my own voice—it sounded thin and harsh. 'Who's that talking?'

'That's a guy's had a hell of a lot of tubes in him in a lot of places,' Hank said. 'Great to see you back with us, Cliff. Nearly lost you a couple of times there.'

'So I heard.'

I told them about hearing the doctors' various pronouncements when they thought I was out of it.

'Scary,' Hank said.

'I didn't see any white light at the end of a tunnel.'

Hank nodded. 'I thought you'd say that.'

'I *knew* you'd say that,' Megan said.

I drew in a deep breath that hurt almost everywhere there was to hurt. I gasped and heard the reedy voice again: 'Tell me.'

'No chance.' Megan pressed the button near the bed. A nurse came in and did something and the mist wrapped around me again.

Out on the hospital balcony the next day, with most of the tubes and hook-ups detached, they told me what had happened. The real name of the man who'd shot me was Cartland. I'd wounded him but not nearly as severely as he had me. He and 'Jones', whose real name was Bolton, and who held a senior position in Lachlan Enterprises, were arrested by the three police officers. When it looked as if I might die and Cartland was facing a murder charge, he made a series of admissions in exchange for the downgrading of the charge to manslaughter. Cartland and an associate, acting on instructions from Bolton, had abducted

Henry McKinley, held and questioned him, as Cartland put
it, 'under duress'. Cartland denied killing him and claimed
McKinley had died of a heart attack. He admitted that he
and his accomplice had torched the car and McKinley's
body.

'Must have been pissed off when I pulled through,'
I said to Hank, who was supplying the details. 'Wounding
at best, and with a good lawyer . . .'

'Right,' Hank said. 'But it unravelled from there.
Bolton named someone higher up in the organisation as the
instigator and he was arrested trying to leave the country.
The press got onto it all from—guess who?'

'Phil Fitzwilliam.'

'Persistent guy, that. They just couldn't keep him at
arm's length. You dealt him a good hand and he played it to
the hilt. He's come out of it OK. Lachlan's shares are in the
toilet.'

'How's Holland, the Global man?'

'In much better shape than you.'

'Tarelton?'

Hank shrugged. 'In serious debt to Lachlan. Christ
knows how that'll sort out. Losing staff is all I heard.'

'Margaret McKinley?'

'We're paid in full.'

'That's not what I meant.'

'She sent flowers. That's it.'

Over the next few weeks as I mended, I had a stream of
visitors and a flow of information. Lachlan's lawyers were
pulling out all the stops for Bolton and the others, and
Hank and I were fending off counter-charges of conspiracy

and entrapment. Hank had hired a high-powered law firm to monitor proceedings and they reported that a stalemate had been reached.

'That's bad,' I said.

Hank said, 'No, apparently that's good. Don't ask me why.'

Margaret emailed Megan for my phone number at the hospital and she called me on a day after I'd completed one of my corridor walks. I was building up towards a couple of hundred metres a day. It was something like the rehab after the heart surgery, but thankfully without the breathing exercises and the elastic stockings.

'You're on the mend Megan tells me.'

'Slowly. How're you?'

'I'm fine. Something to tell you. My ex and I are back together.'

'Your daughter'll be pleased.'

'Is that all you have to say?'

'Margaret, I don't remember any . . . core promises on either side.'

'You're right. I just wanted you to know I won't ever forget what you did for me. For us—for my dad and Lucinda and me, and what you went through to do it.'

'And I'll remember Larson's quarry.'

'Yes,' she said, 'me, too. Goodbye, Cliff.'

The visitors came and went. Patrick Fox-James brought grapes, most of which he ate, throwing them up and catching them in his mouth.

'You done good,' I said.

'Should've thrown myself between you and the bullet.'

DS Angela Roberts came and told me that the .38 I'd used had had one decayed round in the chamber and that I was lucky to have got off a shot at all.

'Always been lucky,' I said.

Josephine Dart, dressed to the nines in silk and with impeccable makeup, tapped her way into the room on her stilettos. She perched on the bed like the late Princess Diana visiting a cancer ward.

'Those people killed my husband, didn't they?' she said.

'Almost certainly, but there'll never be any proof.'

'What did you think of the Myall cottage?'

'Stimulating. Henry's daughter thought the same.'

She stared at me, her violet eyes blinking. 'You didn't.'

'Not exactly,' I said.

My recovery was slow, with setbacks when the infections flared. I fretted at the slowness and the confinement and read the newspapers from first page to last. The Sydney basin aquifer remained sealed, but the drought broke in parts of the state and the city got a lot of rain. There were two pieces of good news: Tony Truscott won the WBA welterweight title, and the outplayed, discredited federal government was emphatically shown the door.

Megan came to collect me on my discharge from the hospital. I'd read a shelf load of books, bought in the Glebe and Newtown second-hand shops by Megan, and I donated them to the hospital library. I signed my name on a batch of forms. My second big hit on the health fund. Well, they'd had a clear run for a long time. I shook hands with the surgeon who'd removed the bullet that had lodged dangerously near my spine.

I said, 'I hope you don't ever need my services, Doctor, but if you do . . .'

'Mr Hardy,' he said, 'you need to lead a quieter life.'